HOLLY AND THE FRAMED FRIEND

A Holly Lewis Mystery Series - Book 1

BY

DIANNE HARMAN

Published by: Dianne Harman
www.dianneharman.com

Interior, cover design and website by
Vivek Rajan

This is a work of fiction. Names, characters, places, and incidents either are the product of the author's imagination or are used fictitiously, and any resemblance to actual persons, living or dead, business establishments, events, or locales, is entirely coincidental.

ISBN: 9781796818444

CONTENTS

ACKNOWLEDGMENTS

Thanks to all the people who allowed me to babysit their children when I was a teenager, so I could spend my earnings on the latest Nancy Drew mysteries.

This series is my homage to all the hours of enjoyment Nancy Drew's mysteries brought me and are probably the reason I write mysteries.

Win **FREE** Paperbacks every week!

Go to www.dianneharman.com/freepaperback.html and get your FREE copies of Dianne's books and favorite recipes immediately by signing up for her newsletter.

Once you've signed up for her newsletter you're eligible to win three paperbacks. One lucky winner is picked every week. Hurry before the offer ends!

PREFACE

As she approached the high school, she pulled on the zip-up hoodie she'd taken from Chloe's room a week earlier. She adjusted the long platinum blonde wig and tugged the large hood up over her head, while at the same time, mentally running through her plan. She'd thought through it a million times before, but finally, this was the day she'd been waiting for to carry out her plan.

This has to work, she thought. *I'm sick and tired of Chloe getting all the attention. She needs to be brought down a peg.*

The plan was fairly simple. The jacket was unique, and everyone knew it was Chloe's. She wore it almost all the time, even when the weather wasn't that cool. It was black with silver stars all over it that her grandmother had hand embroidered. There were no other hoodies like it anywhere, which was just what the vandal was counting on.

By wearing it and a wig that looked like Chloe's own unique hair, she hoped the act of vandalism she was about to commit would be fairly cut and dried. Everyone would think Chloe did it. She knew there were security cameras at each end of the school halls that would record her every movement. All she had to do was keep her face hidden. Everything else should take care of itself.

As she walked up the sidewalk that led to the large brick building,

1

she became aware of just how nervous she was. Although nobody would think twice of a student entering the school building today, since the summer sports kids had a meeting this morning, that didn't mean it felt any less dangerous for her.

She'd planned on getting there early enough so she could enter the school when the doors opened. She didn't want to wait until everyone else started to show up. Anyone who saw her face would be suspicious. After all, why would she, of all people, be wearing Chloe's jacket and a wig?

No, she had to be very, very careful. She'd sat on her bike and watched the last time the summer sports meeting met at the school, so she'd know when the doors would be unlocked and when the majority of the kids would start to arrive. It wasn't a huge window of time, but it should be long enough to do the damage she intended to wreak on Chloe's perfect little world.

She pulled open the glass door that led to the first-floor main hall and paused, listening for sounds. The halls had tile floors, so even the slightest sound echoed. A shoe squeak or a door opening would be easily heard. When no sounds were heard, she made sure the oversized hoodie was pulled all the way forward, so that her face was blocked. She didn't want anyone to see anything but the almost platinum blonde hair and the hoodie, and only one person in school had hair that looked like that. Chloe.

Chloe Sellman was everyone's friend. The teachers loved her as well as the coaches. She was even nice to the janitors and on a first name basis with some of them. That's why the summer bonfire had become so popular. Chloe made friends with everyone, and if you were her friend you were invited. Her parents were there, along with a few other adults, just to keep an eye on things and make sure nothing got out of hand.

It was like a big co-ed camping trip in Chloe's grandparents' field. It had become so popular that even the kids didn't want to screw it up. No one wanted to be the person who messed it up for everyone else, so the majority of them would help keep things clean and keep an eye on their fellow students. It sounded like something out of a television sitcom, but it brought out the best in most people. The bonfire was something everyone looked forward to all year. Everyone loved Chloe and her family for hosting it.

But now she'd decided that Chloe was a little too popular. Maybe it was time for some other people to get some attention, rather than Chloe. It seemed like all the good-looking guys at school had their eyes on Chloe, not that she would ever date anyone. She made it well known she was staying focused on school. *Gag*, the potential vandal thought.

What good was all that popularity if you weren't going to use it to your benefit? And add to that her near perfect grades which she maintained seemingly effortlessly, despite how hard others worked to get them. Plus, she didn't even want to think about how good Chloe was at cross country. If Chloe participated, it was a shoe-in she'd take first place.

The vandal didn't have access to a big tract of land in the country where everyone could party. She was just sick and tired of the huge shadow Chloe Sellman cast across the junior class. Her perfect makeup, perfect family, and perfect grades, were sickening. Surely, she wasn't the only one to feel that way.

Maybe if Chloe didn't look like such a good girl anymore her parents would cancel the summer bonfire. Then, maybe a few other people would get noticed, or at least have a chance. Like her. Yeah, she liked the bonfire as much as the next person. It was fun, but if that had been what helped launch Chloe to fame, then maybe it was the one thing that could topple her.

She pulled out a couple of dry erase markers from her backpack. She wasn't trying to get Chloe in serious trouble. No, just enough trouble to possibly ruin her summer. She just needed a bit of time. She had no intention of getting a criminal record. She wasn't sure if using permanent markers would cause the police to be involved, but if this didn't work, she wasn't sure what the next step would be. She'd have to return the jacket soon, but she'd still have the wig, and she needed to figure out what to do with it.

Starting with the first locker in the row, she began writing swear words and anything else she could come up with. Dirty drawings, trash talking the teachers, there were no limits. She wrote down whatever popped into her mind. Trying to be quick, the letters sprawled across the lockers. Once done with the first floor, she jogged up the stairs and did the same on the second floor.

Her hands shook as she worked, and she didn't know if it was from the fear of getting caught or the pure adrenaline that was pumping through her veins. She wasn't the type who did things like this, but now she understood why the bad kids did the things they did. It was really liberating and the rush was intoxicating.

"Hey, you. Stop!" she heard someone yell. Without looking, she darted in the other direction for the stairs. Since there were three stairways, one on each end, and one in the middle, it made for an easy getaway. It was all a part of the plan, the plan she'd spent so much time thinking about. She was pretty sure she'd been spotted, but that was the point.

The voice sounded like that of the morning janitor. He was an older guy with a big belly and a smoking habit. She doubted he'd be able to chase her for very long. He was always there bright and early, unlocking the doors during the school year, and making sure everything was ready for the school day. She'd been hoping that he'd be the one to spot her.

"Get back here," the person shouted, but there was no way she was stopping now. Not after she'd gone to all the trouble of buying the wig and taking the hoodie. Everything had been planned out perfectly. She'd known what she was doing with every step she'd taken. Now all she had to do was get away.

She slammed through the front door and then burst into a sprint. It was doubtful any teacher or janitor would catch her now. Still, she ran around the corner where she'd hidden her bike. Tugging off the wig and the jacket, she stuffed them into her old grey backpack and slung it over her shoulder. Once on the bike, she pedaled for home.

It wouldn't take long to get there, but with the evidence of the crime sitting in her backpack, she wasn't sure she could relax until it was returned to Chloe's house, unnoticed. The wig would need a permanent hiding spot until she was sure she was done with it. She'd decided that after the bonfire was cancelled, it would be safe to get rid of it. Until then, she needed to keep it around, just in case this didn't do the trick.

The only thing she needed now was a way to get Chloe's jacket back to her without her noticing. That shouldn't be too terribly hard, but it was going to take some planning. As she pedaled toward home, she tried to think of the best way to do it. Once she was a few blocks from school, she slowed down, certain that no one was chasing her.

CHAPTER ONE

Holly Lewis wasn't sure what she expected when she stepped off the airplane and began to make her way through Springfield, Missouri's National Airport. It definitely wasn't anything like the ones she'd seen on television, but she thought that was because those were international airports. Still, for her first time flying, it was overwhelming. She couldn't imagine what it would have been like landing at a bigger airport all alone.

It had been over a year since her mother had been murdered. Ever since that day, her life had changed for the better. It may sound odd to some, but her mother hadn't always been the best mother. Holly had learned to be grateful for those few months toward the end when her mom had been sober.

She'd gotten to see what her mom would have been like without the drugs or alcohol. Because her mom had never done anything in a small way, when she went on a bender, she'd leave Holly alone for days at a time. When Holly had been around seven or eight, she'd had to learn how to make meals for herself, since her mother usually wasn't there to do it.

That was when Holly had first learned to love school. It was the one place where she could be a kid, for at least a little while. Homework had been a welcome respite from the silent walls of the rundown trailer where she and her mother, Maggie, had lived. After her mother's death, Holly had asked a woman named Brigid if she could live with her. Not long before the murder, Brigid had reached out to help Holly and her mother. Brigid had been very involved in assisting the sheriff in finding her mother's killer. It still hurt Holly to think her mother had been murdered in the one place where she'd felt safe. The church.

After her mother was murdered, there'd been no other relatives nearby and the sheriff had told her she'd probably have to leave behind the life she'd known. That was the last thing she'd wanted. After all, who wants to lose everything they'd ever known all at once?

She'd begged him not to make her move to Missouri to live with an aunt she'd never known. Her whole life had been in Cottonwood Springs, Colorado. When Brigid agreed to let Holly move in with her, she'd been so thankful and relieved. Not only was she able to stick around and see that her mother's killer was caught, she was staying in a place where she was happy and felt supported.

Not too long ago, her aunt, Katie McCloud, had reached out to Holly online and expressed an interest in meeting her. She'd asked Holly to come to Springfield to meet her family. She respected that Holly had wanted to stay in the only place she'd ever known, but she wanted to get to know her niece. With Brigid getting married to Linc Olsen, their next-door neighbor, and the two of them leaving on their honeymoon, it seemed like a perfect time to visit her Aunt Katie.

Holly retrieved her suitcase from the luggage carousel and began to look for the area where her Aunt Katie had said she'd be waiting for her. She found a map of the airport and scanned it until she located the "you are here" dot and figured out how to get to the main entrance. Brushing her long blonde hair out of her eyes, she turned in that direction.

She began walking through the small crowd of passengers, intent on finding her aunt. They'd spoken on the phone a few days earlier to clear up any questions the other may have had. Holly had seen a picture of her aunt, uncle, and cousins, so she had a rough idea of what her aunt looked like, but that hadn't prepared her for what she'd feel when she first saw her.

It was almost like looking at a ghost. For a split second, her mind thought she was looking at her mother. Although Katie was a little larger than her mother had been, and since her mother had been very thin, that wasn't hard to do, but they looked strikingly similar. Holly's feet froze, locking her in place for a step before she forced herself to keep moving. She felt her throat tighten up. She'd been wondering what she'd feel like, or if she'd have some sort of reaction to seeing this woman who was the closest living relative to her mother. Holly thought she'd prepared herself, but apparently not well enough.

"Holly?" her aunt asked questioningly. Her chestnut brown hair was longer than her mother's had been. It was a nice length, half-way down her back similar to the way Holly wore her hair. It was parted on the side and the highlights that had been added gave her a brighter look. Her aunt even had the same crooked crease that appeared between her eyebrows when she was concerned, just like her mother had.

When Katie smiled, Holly felt tears begin to trickle down from the corners of her eyes. For the first time, Holly wondered if she'd prepared herself well enough emotionally for this occasion. She'd been through a lot in her fourteen years, but nothing prepared her for facing her mother's ghost.

Holly nodded and was grateful that, as she drew closer, the similarities between her aunt and mother became less pronounced. Katie had slight differences that were obvious now that she could see her close up. For one thing, their eyes were a different color. Katie looked softer than her mother had looked and had a naturally kind expression on her face.

Opening her arms, she greeted Holly with a hug. "I'm sorry, I'm a hugger," she said as she pulled her in. When she stepped back there were tears in her eyes. "You look just like Maggie did when she was a young girl," she said softly.

"Thank you," Holly said. She wasn't sure what she should say to that, considering she didn't know why her mother had hardly ever spoken of her sister. For a moment, Holly wondered if her mom would be angry or happy that she'd gone to visit her aunt.

"Well, everyone's waiting for us back home. Let's get out of here," she said, taking Holly's suitcase. She followed her aunt outside and into the warm sun. Missouri wasn't that much different than Colorado. The trees were different and there weren't any mountains in the distance, but if you didn't look very closely, they were almost the same.

Holly walked with her aunt through the rows of cars gleaming in the morning sun. Finally, Katie stopped at a newer looking minivan and pushed a button on her keys. The sliding door popped open. "Let's toss your things in the back, and you can ride up front with me," she said.

After they'd climbed into the minivan and Katie had navigated her way out of the parking lot, she said, "We've added a few things to our guest bedroom for you. There's a flat screen and a laptop you can use while you're here. If there's anything else you need, anything at all while you're here, you let me know," she insisted.

"I will," Holly said, nodding. She looked out the window at the traffic going by. "The only big city I've ever been to is Denver," she admitted.

"You're going to love Springfield," Katie said with a smile. "There's just about something for everyone here. It's great. Are you into museums, art, sports, music? Any of it? I know you said you read a lot, but surely you play some kind of sport or something?"

"Not really," Holly said. "Mom never had the money for uniforms or equipment. The only sports I played were in gym class."

Katie was quiet a moment, as if she were trying to decide how to respond. Finally, she said, "Well, I guess we can just see what sounds fun to you."

Holly was a little weirded out by what she thought was Katie's overly chipper attitude, and she had a feeling it was an act. Not that she was a fake, but just that she was trying to seem overly warm and friendly, so Holly wouldn't feel awkward. It had to be just as weird for her as it was for Holly, and she was glad her aunt was trying so hard.

"Sounds like fun," she said smiling, and it did. Holly was looking forward to seeing what all Springfield had to offer. Maybe, if she enjoyed herself here, she could get Linc and Brigid to come visit next time. Of course, first she'd have to decide how she felt about these people that were now her "family." She watched Katie when she wasn't looking and while the woman seemed kind and nice, there had to be a reason her mother had stopped speaking to her. The question was, why?

CHAPTER TWO

As soon as Holly climbed out of the minivan the front door of the large brick home opened. It was a two-story house that was square with the exception of the carport area that jutted out from the side of the house. A winding sidewalk led from the driveway up to the front door. Seasonal flowers swayed in a slight breeze. She wasn't quite sure what they were, but the whole thing was beautiful. She didn't know exactly what she'd expected, but it definitely wasn't this.

A man and two teenagers had come out of the house and stood around while they waited for her to get her things. "Holly, this is your Uncle Allen and your cousins, Lissa and Steven," Katie said.

"Hey," Holly made a short little wave to them, feeling awkward.

"It's great to meet you, Holly," Allen said. He stepped forward and shook her hand politely. He was a tall man, well over six feet. His hair, which was a light brown, was cut short on the sides, but the top was longer and styled. He was wearing modern black glasses and was dressed a bit like those stylish dads you see in the catalogs with his olive-green shirt and brown slacks. "We've tried to plan a quiet evening, so you can get your bearings."

"Thanks, I appreciate that," Holly said. She wasn't used to being surrounded by people who were strangers. All day she'd found herself looking around for a familiar face, before realizing she was in a completely new place and there wouldn't be any.

"It's cool getting another cousin our age," Lissa said to her. She looked to be about Holly's age. Her long dark brown hair hung in waves and was pinned back on one side. Her eyes reminded Holly of Katie and her mom's. Somehow that made her relax a little. She was wearing a Johnny Cash t-shirt under a short-sleeved plaid shirt and cut-off denim shorts.

Steven was almost as tall as his dad and seemed a bit older. "Could have used another boy in the family, but you'll do," he said grinning playfully.

Holly laughed and said, "Sorry to disappoint." She felt the tension in her neck ease, realizing they were probably just as nervous about meeting her as she was about meeting them. They were trying hard, just like she was.

"Well, let's get Holly inside and unpacked," Katie said. "Steven, why don't you carry her suitcase up the stairs? Lissa, will you show her where her room and everything is?"

"Sure. Follow me, Holly," Lissa said with a wave as she turned and walked inside.

Stepping through the big wooden front door, Holly was a little taken aback. Brigid's house was lovely, but this place was big, old and beautiful. Both were nice, but in completely different ways. This place felt like it had been home to many generations. The hardwood floors shined in the entry and a sparkling chandelier hung from the ceiling. The stairs were against the wall on the right with a dark cherry wood finish. It was old, and yet modern, all at the same time. For Holly, it seemed like a great place to learn about her family history.

Lissa dashed up the wooden stairs. Holly shook herself and followed. Each step creaked as she followed her cousin to what would be her room for the next two weeks.

On the second floor, Lissa took a right and opened the first door. "This is your room. Mom and I picked out a new bedspread and curtains for you. Honestly, the other ones were kind of blah. Trust me, I did you a favor," she said as she touched Holly's forearm with exaggerated sympathy.

"Thanks," Holly said, not completely sure what else she could say. "So how old are you again?"

"I'm 13. I'll be a freshman next year," she said as she walked over to the closet. Pulling the door open she did a fancy move like she was on a game show. "This is your closet, my dear."

Holly laughed. "The only thing I can think about right now is finding a bathroom. Would you show me where it is?" She'd needed to go ever since she'd been on the airplane, but she hadn't wanted to squeeze into the tiny compartment on the plane.

"Sure. Come on, I'll show you that before I give you a tour of the rest of the house." Lissa bounced out of the room and down the hall.

Holly secretly hoped the girl was just excited she was here. She wasn't sure if she could handle being around someone so perky all the time. It wasn't natural.

When she was finished in the bathroom, Lissa showed her the upstairs rooms before taking her back down the stairs. She stopped in front of a nearby door.

"This is my dad's office. He works from home," Lissa explained.

"That's cool, so does Brigid. What does he do?" Holly asked.

"He's a web developer. He builds websites and stuff," Lissa said proudly. "Brigid's the woman you live with, right? What does she do?"

"Yeah, she's taken care of me since Mom died. She's a book editor," Holly said as Lissa pushed the door open.

Allen was sitting behind his desk, his face illuminated by a computer screen. "Hey, Lissa, giving Holly the grand tour?" he asked.

"Sure am," Lissa said smiling proudly.

"Why don't you take her to the kitchen? She may want a snack or something," he suggested.

The girls began to chat as they walked through the house towards the kitchen. Katie had already set out some snacks for them.

"Is your room okay?" Katie asked.

Holly nodded as she picked up a chocolate chip cookie and took a small bite. "Yes, thank you. You really didn't need to go to all that trouble for me," she said. "Whatever you had before would have been fine."

"It wasn't any trouble at all. That guest room needed a change, and having you visit gave us a good reason to do it. Well, I'm going to go out and check on the garden. You kids can watch television or play a game, or whatever. Make yourself at home, Holly. If you need anything, just let someone know."

She smiled brightly as she stepped through the French doors that led out to the backyard. Holly looked out at the view. The backyard was a decent size, not nearly as big as theirs back in Cottonwood Springs, but still not bad for being in the middle of a city.

It was fenced-in and nicely landscaped. Right outside the doors was a large stone patio with a table and chairs. There was also a little fire pit nearby. Holly could almost imagine them all sitting around it roasting hot dogs or marshmallows.

Steven walked into the kitchen and headed straight for the chocolate chip cookies. "So, has everyone driven you nuts yet with their constant chatter?" he asked jokingly.

"Not yet," Holly laughed. "But I do have to admit that I'm not used to all of this attention."

Steven sat down on a barstool at the edge of the large island in the middle of the kitchen and pulled the cookies closer to him. "You'll get used to it. They just want you to be happy," he said. He didn't make a lot of eye contact, because he was focused on the cookies.

Lissa pulled out a barstool for Holly before sitting down herself. "Well, duh. We don't want her to be miserable while she's here," she said as if he was being an idiot.

"I'm not used to much. I can make myself happy just about anywhere with a good book and something to eat," Holly said as she snagged another cookie.

"Reader, huh? Does that mean you don't play video games?" Steven asked.

"Honestly, I've only played a few times over at friends' houses," she admitted.

"What?" Lissa asked, turning towards Holly with wide eyes. "You have got to be joking. You don't have some sort of gaming system?"

"Well, no. My mom didn't have a lot of money, and since I've never really had one, I didn't ask Brigid for one," Holly said, but it wasn't like she didn't know what they were or anything.

"We'll change that," Steven said. "You have got to play something while you're here." He turned to his sister and shook his head. "A teenager who doesn't play video games. It's just not right."

Lissa giggled as Holly rolled her eyes while she smiled. She was already starting to like having cousins.

CHAPTER THREE

Allison had been checking the school website for her grade point average and the class ranking list which told everyone which five students had the top GPAs. It was the summer before her senior year, and she was determined to be named valedictorian. She had the grades for it, and she'd been working hard to make sure her GPA stayed as high as possible. It wasn't just her dream to be valedictorian, it was also her mother's.

Her mother had been forced to drop out of school when she'd become pregnant with Allison. A complicated pregnancy and all the stress that went with it had made it almost impossible to keep her attendance and grades up. When Allison had started high school, her mother confided in her one night that she dreamed her daughter would be valedictorian, fulfilling her unmet dream of years ago.

"My grades were almost perfect," she'd admitted. "I wouldn't change having you for the world, but when I started having troubles with my pregnancy my grades slipped, because of all the doctors' appointments and days when I couldn't get out of bed. It wasn't long before my perfect GPA went down the drain."

Seeing the sadness in her eyes had done something to Allison. All her life it had been just the two of them. They were like two peas in a pod, always there for each other. Knowing what her mother had gone through to raise her the best way she could made Allison want to make her mother proud of her. She wanted her mother to feel that all of the sacrifices she'd made had paid off.

"If I couldn't be valedictorian, I'd love to see you be it. You have the grades, and you're definitely smart enough. That would be like me getting it after all these years," her mother had said, growing misty-eyed.

"I'll do it for you, you'll see," Allison had promised her. Her mother had smiled and patted her hand before heading off to her second job as a waitress. That night Allison mentally swore that she would do whatever she could to make sure she didn't let her mother down.

Now they were getting down to the wire. Her grades had been good during her first three years of high school, but Chloe consistently had the best grades. No matter how hard Allison tried, it was never quite enough. She just hoped that maybe, just maybe, all the extra studying she'd done would pay off. If she tried to work on the subjects over the summer, she hoped she could get a leg up for next year's courses and beat out Chloe.

She clicked on the link to show the class standings, holding her breath and crossing her fingers. Looking above the computer, she smiled at the picture of her mother and her that was taken last year. They both had the same caramel-colored skin and straight brown hair. Allison's was a bit lighter than her mom's, but not much.

They'd gone to the park for a picnic on one of her mother's rare days off. It wasn't often that they were able to do much together. Working two jobs, her mother was usually trying to catch up on sleep or things that she thought needed to be done around the house whenever she had a day off.

"I've got this," she said to the picture. She wasn't sure if she was talking more to herself or to her mother. Either way, she had to think positively.

When the page loaded, she eagerly looked at the top of the list, certain she would see her name there this time. Instead, it was the same as always. Chloe. Right beneath her name was Allison's name.

"Darn!" Allison yelled, slamming her hands down on the desk. What would it take to beat her? Was it even possible? It was as if Chloe was a robot who'd been sent to destroy all of Allison's dreams.

Standing up from the desk, she paced back and forth in the small, square front room. There wasn't much space between the old couch, the coffee table, and the television, but she managed. She was used to moving around the furniture in their tiny home.

"It's not fair," she said aloud to the pale grey walls. "Why can't I ever beat her?" She'd been trying so hard, giving it her best. Each time, no matter how much extra credit or studying she did, Chloe was always just a little farther ahead.

Frustrated, she looked at the time and realized her mother would be home soon. Sighing, she walked over to the computer and turned it off. "There's got to be something I can do. Maybe if I keep it up, she'll slip," she said as she thought out loud. "She's not perfect. She's human, just like me. There's no way she can keep this up forever."

Heading to the kitchen, she opened the old refrigerator and pulled out the ingredients to make sandwiches. It wasn't much, but she didn't have time to make anything else. Her mom would only be home an hour and a half before heading to her other job. Allison had made it her job to make sure her mother took care of herself. She had a habit of forgetting to eat, among other things.

Allison had taken over most of the housework as well as making dinner. She knew other kids her age didn't have to do those things, but she didn't care. She'd do anything to try to help her mother out. Cooking dinner and helping around the house was nothing compared to the long hours her mom had to put in just to keep a roof over their head and food in the refrigerator.

Allison's dream was to get into a good college on a full ride scholarship. She wanted to study psychology and help people work through their problems. She was still trying to decide if she wanted to specialize, but she knew that was something she could decide later. Right now, all she knew was that she wanted to make a difference.

After college, she wanted to take care of her mother, buy her a house, and make sure she didn't ever have to work again. Allison wasn't sure how she was going to manage all that, but she knew her own needs would come second this time. For so many years she'd watched as her mom went without so Allison could have things.

The sound of a key sliding into the lock on the front door brought Allison out of her thoughts.

"Hey, Mama. How was work?" she asked as her mother stepped through the front door and shut it behind her.

"Exhausting. What do you have there?" She crossed the short distance from the front door to the kitchen counter that separated it from the living area.

"A ham and swiss cheese sandwich. Here, have some chips, too," she said as she pulled a bag from the cabinet and put a handful on a plate with the sandwich. She'd made the sandwich just the way her mother liked, with double cheese and lettuce right in the middle.

"You are too good to me, sweetheart," she said, her voice sounding tired. There were dark circles under her eyes, and she looked a little pale.

"Sit down and eat. Kick off your shoes and relax," Allison insisted.

Without arguing, her mother shuffled over to the couch. *She must be tired*, Allison thought. *That's the only time she doesn't argue with me and try to help.* Her heart broke for her mother. It couldn't be healthy for her to work this hard.

"I think I may go to the library later on," Allison said as she made her own sandwich. "I know it's summer vacation, but I got a list of the required reading for next year's courses from one of my friends who graduated. If I read them ahead of time, maybe I'll have a leg up when we study them this year," she continued.

"If I have time, I'll probably try to find out the algebraic equations that will be introduced and see if the library has any videos on them." Placing a handful of chips on her own plate, she got a glass of ice water and left the kitchen.

She sat down on the couch and looked over at her mother, who had already fallen asleep. Her chips were almost all gone and half the sandwich was eaten. Her head was tipped back against the couch and her mouth had dropped slightly open. A gentle soft snore coming from her was the only sound in the room.

Allison felt a pang of guilt. Her mother was working herself into the ground for her. No matter how much Allison insisted it would be okay, her mother wouldn't listen. She was forever trying to work just a little more, so she could put money away in Alison's college fund.

Allison had assured her mother she'd be able to get some sort of scholarship or grants, and that she didn't need to work so hard. But her mother wanted to make sure everything was covered, so she kept at it, even when she was practically asleep on her feet.

Carefully, Allison slid the plate from her mother's lap and set it on the table. It would keep for a little while. No reason why she couldn't rest a bit. She pulled the quilt from the back of the couch and softly whispered, "Lie down, Mom. It's okay. I'll wake you up in time to get to work."

Mumbling her thanks, her mother lifted her feet onto the couch and scooted down. Her wrinkled scrubs rode up on her calves. Allison tugged them down before covering her with the quilt. Alison's grandmother had made it for her mother when she was just a small child. Now it was the only thing her mother had left of her mother's. It was one of her most prized possessions.

Once again, Allison promised herself that this wouldn't go on forever. She'd do whatever it took to take first place away from Chloe. For her, getting that spot meant everything would finally be okay. Granted, it didn't promise a scholarship or anything like that, but in her mind, it was almost guaranteed if she beat Chloe in the race for highest GPA.

But what if she still beats me? Allison thought. *What if, no matter what I do, she's just better?* Taking her plate to her room, she sat down on her bed and took a bite of her sandwich.

"Then I just have to make sure she messes up," she whispered to herself. "But how?"

She began to think that the best way to get someone to have bad grades was to distract them. But nothing could fluster Chloe, could it? After all, it was well-known she wouldn't even date because she didn't want anything to make her lose her focus on becoming a pediatrician.

"But what if she was to get in trouble?" she speculated. "Not only would she be distracted, but her perfect reputation would be tarnished. It could mess with her mind and cause her to slip up in her grades," she plotted aloud. Allison knew it wasn't exactly right, but desperate times called for desperate measures. Of course, she didn't want to get Chloe in serious trouble, but maybe just a little trouble. She didn't want to risk the police getting involved. But maybe, just maybe, if she did the right thing and made it reasonably look like Chloe did it...

A smile spread across her lips. Now she just needed a plan.

CHAPTER FOUR

It was dinner time and everyone was seated around the dining room table. The dining room wasn't like most of the traditional dining rooms Holly had seen in magazines or on television that always seemed to look stuffy to Holly. The walls were covered with pictures of the family, places they'd been, things like that.

There were a lot of people Holly didn't recognize, and she wondered if these strangers were also related to her. It still blew her mind that she could be related to so many people and have no clue who any of them were. It was kind of like there was this entire family out there with a hole in it where she was supposed to be.

"This is really good," Holly said politely. While Katie didn't cook nearly as well as Linc, the man Brigid had married, she still did a very good job. Dinner may just have been homemade burgers and fries, but they were possibly the best Holly had ever eaten.

"Thank you, it's kind of an old secret recipe. Did you have anything special you liked for your mom to cook? Or maybe Brigid?" Katie asked.

"Mom never really cooked for me," Holly said, shifting uncomfortably in her chair. "She'd make stuff like hot dogs or whatever, but nothing like this. Brigid and her new husband, Linc, can really cook," Holly said appreciatively.

"I can't believe Maggie stopped cooking," Katie said shaking her head. Her voice held a touch of sadness, as if Maggie not cooking was such a terrible thing.

"What do you mean?" Holly asked. She couldn't imagine someone being surprised that her mother had stopped cooking.

"She used to always want to cook. As a matter of fact, Maggie did a lot of the cooking when we were growing up, because she really loved it. Sometimes she'd go to the library and check out cookbooks. Of course, this was before all that stuff was on the internet. Back then, if you wanted a recipe, you needed to have a cookbook," she said as she ate.

"Wow," Holly said, trying to imagine her mother loving to cook. She remembered plenty of times when her mother was drunk and she'd just toss a box of macaroni and cheese to Holly when she'd ask what they were having for dinner. How could someone who was opposed to even boiling water have loved cooking?

"She started taking a cooking class when she was around sixteen or seventeen. It wasn't long after that she left," Katie said.

"Why did she leave?" Holly asked. "Whenever I'd ask her, she'd just start complaining about how nobody would listen to her, and that her family had abandoned her."

"I'm not sure," Katie said suddenly looking away. She lifted her napkin and dabbed at the corners of her mouth. "Allen, how's the latest project going?" she asked, clearly changing the subject.

"Not too bad," he began. "The client's having a tough time deciding on a few things, but I think we'll get them hammered out in another day or so. Truthfully, I'll be happy to see this one in my rearview mirror," he continued.

Holly watched Katie as she listened intently to Allen. It was obvious the question of her mother's leaving made her feel uncomfortable. But why? Why would both sisters want to avoid the same question? Holly had a feeling this went much deeper than she'd ever realized.

Perhaps, while she was visiting, she could find the answer to why she'd grown up without a family. What reason did her mother have for leaving her family behind and moving to Colorado? And how did she end up in Cottonwood Springs, of all places?

These were all things Holly had wondered about before, but especially after her mother had died. It wasn't that she'd never wondered about them before, but she was normally too mad at her mother for being high on drugs and ignoring her. But in the time since then, she'd become curious as to what had made her mother the person she was. And who had she been before?

"Are you going to visit Grandpa while you're here?" Lissa asked Holly.

"Grandpa?" Holly asked in a confused tone of voice.

"I didn't tell her about him, Lissa," Katie interrupted. She turned to Holly, "I wasn't trying to hide anything from you, but I just didn't know how overwhelmed you might be with us and a new place. I wanted you to get acclimated first. If you aren't ready to meet him, that's fine. I haven't told him you were visiting, just in case."

Katie looked worried. Holly wondered if it was more about the fact she hadn't said anything before, or because she didn't really want Holly to meet him. She could see that Katie was visibly nervous.

"And he's my mom's and your father?" she asked.

"Yes, he even lives in the same house we grew up in," Katie admitted. "Mom died a long time ago."

If Holly hadn't been sitting down, she was pretty sure she would have needed to. "I knew my grandmother died a long time ago, but I never dreamed I'd get a chance to meet my grandfather. I'd love to meet him," she said softly, her voice cracking. She cleared her throat.

"If that's okay."

"Sure," Katie said smiling. "I'll give him a call later on and let him know you're here before we go over there. He's not as young as he used to be."

Holly nodded. "Is there any other family around?" she asked.

"Not really," Allen said as he finished his burger. "There are some a few hours away from here, but they're more your mother's cousins and extended family. A while back we lived a ways from here, but we decided to move back so we could be closer to your grandfather."

Holly's brain was still swimming with the thought of meeting her grandfather. She didn't know why, but she'd always kind of assumed he'd passed away. It had never crossed her mind he could still be around, let alone in the same home her mother had grown up in. Seeing where her mom had lived was too much to resist.

Once everyone was finished with dinner, Steven asked Holly if she wanted to play a game.

"Do you guys have board games?" Holly asked.

"I think so," he said. "But I kind of meant a video game."

"Oh," Holly said. "Well, this is the night that Brigid and I usually played a board game when I was back in Colorado. It's this stupid thing we started when I moved in with her," she said, letting her sentence trail off.

"Then you guys should definitely play one together. There's a few in the upstairs closet," Allen said. "I'd love to join you, but I need to wrap a few things up. Katie? If you aren't busy could you give me your designer eye for a moment?" They headed for his office while Steven, Lissa, and Holly went upstairs.

"I'm not going to lie. It's been a long time since I played something like this," Steven admitted.

"It'll be fun. Trust me," Holly said.

CHAPTER FIVE

Carrie felt her cell phone vibrate in her pocket. Pulling it out, she saw it was her friend, Kyle.

I heard there's going to be fireworks at the bonfire this year, Kyle messaged.

Carrie swiped across her screen to open the message. *That's cool,* she typed. It wasn't what she wanted to say, but for now she had to keep that to herself.

I think I'm finally going to make a play for Chloe, he replied.

Why? She's just going to shoot you down, she responded as she tucked her phone back in her pocket. She was sitting with her family watching some movie on television, the name of which she couldn't even remember.

"I'm going to my room," Carrie said as she stood up. Her mother nodded and told her she could take some popcorn with her if she'd like to.

"No thanks," she said as she disappeared. Now, just thinking about the way Kyle fell all over Chloe, made her feel like throwing up.

Carrie Fox was friends with Chloe, but that didn't mean she was her biggest fan. Maybe she had been a while ago, but that was before Kyle decided he had a crush on Chloe. Carrie couldn't fathom why he liked Chloe. It was probably just a case of wanting something he couldn't have. Carrie was sure that was the reason why most of the guys liked her.

Pushing open her bedroom door, she let it softly click shut behind her. Carrie really wasn't sure if she had it in her to hear Kyle talk about Chloe again, even if it was just through a text. When he hadn't responded, she wondered if maybe her response had sounded too callous, but in a few minutes he replied.

But there has to be a way to get through that shield of hers. You're her friend. HELP ME!

Why do you like her so much, anyway? she sent back. Carrie took a long look at herself in the mirror. She'd been told she was pretty on multiple occasions. Maybe she wasn't as tall or thin as Chloe, but this was the modern age. The era of the blonde bombshell was over, wasn't it? Can't shorter, slightly curvy brunettes get the guy, too?

Of course, Kyle had no clue. How could he? Carrie hadn't ever told him how she felt. They'd grown up together and had been hanging out since the first grade. It wasn't until they were in the sixth grade that Carrie realized she had a crush on Kyle.

Back then, he'd been a little on the chubby side with cute little pinchable cheeks and braces. Freckles covered his nose, and he had short brown hair that looked almost golden in sunlight. Carrie moved to her desk where there was a mirror hanging above it. There, slipped into the frame, was one of many photographs of the two of them hanging out. This one was when they'd ridden their bikes to the park and had hung out there all day, just talking. It had to be almost four years ago. She pulled the photo out of the frame and gently caressed Kyle's picture.

It snuck up on Carrie at first. She didn't realize she liked him that way until one day it hit her like a ton of bricks. She'd been sitting on the couch playing some racing game at his house. She looked over at him and suddenly he wasn't the guy she'd grown up with. He was a man. She saw it in his jawline, the sharp curve of his nose. His shoulders were broader and his arms were becoming muscular and well-defined.

Sliding the photograph back in the frame, Carrie couldn't help but feel responsible for Kyle falling for Chloe. He'd gotten to know Chloe from the times Carrie visited her. It was only a couple of times, but that was all it took.

Because she's so nice and sweet. Plus, she's super smart, he finally responded in a text message.

Carrie made a rude noise before flopping down on her fluffy turquoise comforter. She hated it when he started telling her just how awesome he thought Chloe was.

Gag me, she typed back.

Haven't you ever liked someone and just wanted them to notice you? he texted back.

Her fingers hovered over the keypad. She really wanted to tell him, "Yes, you, you big oaf!" but she couldn't. It wasn't like she hadn't tried over and over again. The moment would be there, and she'd think this is the time for me to tell him. But then she'd wait too long and things would either get awkward, or he'd be so oblivious he'd start talking about something else.

Yes, was all she sent in her reply text message. Laying her phone on her chest she looked up at the white popcorn acoustic ceiling.

Do you like someone now? he sent back.

Here it was, another moment. If only she could seize it. Her soft mint walls felt as though they were pressing in all around her. The blood rushed in her ears as her brain began to tingle with anticipation. Her heart began to beat fast as she typed out, "it's you" before erasing it and simply sending, *Yeah.*

Then maybe we both need to stop being so chicken and put ourselves out there, he said.

She wanted to scream and throw her phone across the room, even though she knew it wouldn't do any good. Shattering her phone wasn't going to make Kyle have any feelings for her.

Carrie wished it were possible. She wished there was a chance he'd notice her as more than just a friend. But as the years went on, she'd finally given up that hope. Now, all that was left was an aching sadness as she watched him pine for her friend.

She was starting to feel restless. Maybe Kyle was right. Maybe, before she felt completely hopeless, she should put herself out there. Let him see that she was interested. As soon as the thought crossed her mind, it was filled with images of Chloe. It was as though her brain was showing her that she was the complete opposite of her.

So she couldn't really compete with Chloe, but what if Chloe wasn't a factor anymore? Kyle was always going on and on about how smart Chloe was and how she was such a good person. It was like he thought Chloe was some sort of perfect princess sent down from on high to live with the common folk. But what if there was a way to make her look less than perfect? Surely that would make him see her differently. Perhaps even end his crazy infatuation with her.

Maybe something could happen so that Chloe wouldn't look quite so wonderful. Carrie didn't hate Chloe, and she didn't want to do anything too terrible. Just something bad enough to make her look a little less wonderful in everyone's eyes, particularly Kyle's, but was that even possible?

Carrie was sure with just a smidge of creativity, she could come up with something and make it look like Chloe had done it. Then she'd lose her good girl image and Kyle would have to question if she was even who he thought she was. Carrie could step in and show him just how awesome she was. How she knew his favorite snack, favorite movie, all those little things that made Kyle who he was. If she knocked Chloe off her pedestal, maybe Kyle would open his eyes and see who had been right in front of him the entire time. Carrie.

That was it. She'd make Chloe look less like Miss Perfect and be there to let Kyle down softly. Then, she'd make her move. It wasn't foolproof yet, but it would be. She'd already thought of doing something like this before, but she'd never felt that determined. Maybe the time had come.

CHAPTER SIX

"Was it just me or was Mom totally avoiding Holly's question?" Lissa asked after they'd set up the Monopoly game in her room. They'd considered setting it up downstairs, but decided it would be better to be away from the adults for a while. Katie had already made them stop playing once so they could help with a few chores. Once they'd had the chance to escape, they had.

Holly had been taking in the movie posters that hung on the almost turquoise walls in Lissa's room. It definitely looked like a teenager's room. Books were scattered everywhere, and clothes were on every surface. It was refreshing.

"I noticed it too," Steven admitted. "That's not like her at all."

"Really?" Holly asked. "I just assumed she never talked about any of it."

"That's the thing," Steven began. "She's normally extremely open about everything. She's a big believer in not keeping secrets. Has been for as long as I can remember. I've never seen her act cagey like that. Something's up."

"But why not just answer? And why would she not tell Grandpa?" Lissa asked. "Why wouldn't Grandpa want to see Holly?"

Holly had been wondering the same thing. She'd been telling herself since dinner that maybe it was just the way things were here. After all, she didn't know them that well. Who's to say they weren't a secretive family? But now she knew that Lissa and Steven had noticed it, too.

"So you're saying, this kind of thing is not the norm around here?" she asked.

"Definitely not," Steven insisted. "Of course, I don't know that anyone has ever tried to talk to her about Aunt Maggie. It's always been one of those subjects we didn't talk about. Like, we knew it would upset her, so we just avoided it completely."

"Hmm," Holly said. "If I were back home, I'd ask Brigid for her investigative skills. I mean, it's not like I haven't done my own share of investigating...," she trailed off.

"What do you mean?" Lissa asked.

"Brigid has helped our local sheriff with a few investigations here and there. I pretty much know how she does it. I even caught a student at my school who posted this mean picture of one of the teachers. Surely figuring out what's going on in the family shouldn't be too hard?"

Holly was starting to feel as though this was something that needed to be uncovered. Buried secrets weren't healthy in a family. She didn't want anyone else to be hurt or suffer if they didn't need to. What if her mother hadn't felt as though she'd been abandoned by her family? The thought of piecing it all together excited Holly, but she was going to need help.

"How can we help?" Steven asked, determined.

"I'm not completely sure right now," Holly admitted. "We need to think this through." She began chewing on the inside of her cheek as she tried to imagine the best way to start.

"Lissa, do you have some sort of notebook? Maybe we can compare the stories that we've heard about what happened and see if there's anything that doesn't add up. By the way, I don't know if Katie told you, but she's not really my mom," Steven said.

"No, she didn't."

"My mother died not too long after she had me. Dad met Katie and they got married. Lissa is Katie's and dad's daughter, but Katie has always treated me as if I was her biological son. She's really pretty cool."

"Thanks for telling me," Holly said. "Lissa, what about a notebook?"

"I'll get it," she said as she stood up and went over to her desk. Pulling open one drawer after another, she finally found a spare spiral notebook and a pen.

"What do you know about why my mom left or what have you been told?" Holly asked. She never imagined that there could possibly be two sides to the story. How would she feel if she found out her mother had been in the wrong?

When she was younger, she'd have tea parties all alone, dreaming of having her grandparents, cousins, and other family members be there. It was so lonely growing up, and it would hurt if she found out her mom had taken the opportunity away just because of some argument or whatever. There had to be a much bigger reason why she left and never went back.

"Well, she never really talked much about it. Actually, she didn't talk about Maggie at all until I saw her picture in a photo album over at Grandpa's," Steven began. "I was doing a family history project and needed some older photos. At first, I thought maybe it was a cousin or something, but I asked Grandpa and he told me it was Mom's sister, Maggie."

"That's right," Lissa said nodding. She was writing things down in the notebook. "I remember that."

Steven nodded. "Yeah, I asked Mom when we got home and she admitted to having a sister. When I asked her why she'd never said anything, she just said it had never come up."

"How could the fact she had a sister just 'never come up'?" Holly asked.

"My thoughts exactly," Steven said. "But I could tell it made her uncomfortable, so I never asked again. It wasn't until your mom died that there was a real discussion about her." He shrugged his shoulders and took his turn to roll the dice in the monopoly game.

"What were you told?" Lissa asked Holly as she turned the page in the notebook and then took her turn to roll the dice.

"Honestly, I don't know much. All I know was we had a picture hanging in our trailer that was of my mom, your mom, and their mom. It was taken not long before my mother left Springfield. She told me she moved to Colorado and not long after that, Grandma died. Shortly after that, she said your mom moved away, too." Holly tried to recall if her mother had ever mumbled anything else.

Sometimes when she was more drunk than stoned, she would open up and talk. It wasn't very often, but it had happened once or twice. Unfortunately, it never lasted long, and Holly never really got a whole lot out of her. It sounded like her mother reacted the same way Katie had.

"I think I might have overheard something like that once, that Grandma died not long before our mom moved to St. Louis," Steven nodded. "That's where Katie and my dad met. We lived there when we were younger."

"What was your mom like?" Lissa asked Holly, truly curious.

"My mom wasn't like yours," Holly sighed. "She wasn't around a lot. Alcohol and drugs kept her busy most of the time. When I was really little, she'd pawn me off to pretty much anyone who lived nearby and would agree to watch me.

One time, when she couldn't find anyone, she decided I was old enough to stay by myself. When the trailer didn't burn down the first couple of times she left me, she started staying away for longer periods of time. Eventually, she'd often be gone for a week or so at a time." Holly felt her chest begin to ache just remembering it. "I was probably around eight or nine when I first stayed alone."

"Whoa," Lissa said. "I still barely get left alone, and I'm thirteen."

"Mom and Dad still don't like to leave the two of us alone and I'm seventeen," Steven said in a surprised tone of voice.

Holly shrugged. "Trust me, I'd have rather not been left alone. She wasn't exactly known for keeping the house clean or doing grocery shopping. I don't even know if I'd still be alive if it hadn't been for some of my teachers."

"I wish you would have been closer," Lissa said. "Our mom would have made sure you were taken care of."

"Isn't that the truth?" Steven scoffed. "She's like the ultimate helicopter mom. She's always around trying to help." He made a high-pitched voice, "Do you need something? Did you take your vitamin? You look pale, maybe you should rest."

The girls giggled at his impersonation.

"That's sweet," Holly said smiling. "Brigid's not that bad. She takes care of me, but she also lets me have my space. I really got lucky with her."

"Good," Steven said. "So how did you end up with her anyway? Mom tried to explain it to me, but I didn't really get it."

As the board game continued, Holly told them the story of how her mom had started to get sober and clean up her act. Then she told them everything that happened after that to bring her to where she was today. She told them about Missy, Linc, and Fiona, the bookstore, and everyone else in Cottonwood Springs. Describing them all, she realized just how much they were all her family. None of them might be blood-related, but they had shown Holly what real love and loyalty looked like.

"And now you have family that's blood-related, too," Lissa said brightly.

Holly smiled. "To be honest, it's still kind of strange."

"Don't worry about it. I don't know about everyone else, but Lissa and I are here for you. I can promise you that. We'll do everything we can to help you figure out exactly why your mom left and why our mom tried to brush it under the rug," Steven proclaimed.

"I really appreciate that," Holly said. The tightness in her chest had been slowly releasing after thinking about her family in Cottonwood Springs, but hearing words of support from the cousins she'd just met made her feel much more at ease and wanted. She hadn't realized it, but part of her had been worried that maybe no one had really wanted her to come to Springfield and she'd been asked because her aunt thought it was the right thing to do. It was nice to know that wasn't the case. "Now, who's ready to pay me some money?" she asked as they returned to their game.

CHAPTER SEVEN

Stephanie was tired of always being in Chloe's shadow. Not only was she extremely smart and pretty, but she was one of the fastest runners on the girls cross country team. Even though the meets were over for the year, the girls got together and trained all summer. Today, they'd met at the park and were running along their usual practice path that went around the perimeter of the park.

Although it wasn't Stephanie's favorite place to run, it would do for today. She knew that running on an unfamiliar trail while her mind was occupied could be bad for her. It was far better to let the mind wander when you were somewhere you knew like the back of your hand. Otherwise, a sprained ankle or something worse could sideline her.

"How's it going, Steph?" Abigail asked as she caught up to her.

"Not too bad," Stephanie said easily. Even though Abigail was one of the slower runners on the team, she could always go the distance. Her curly dark hair was pulled back in a ponytail that was looped through her baseball style hat.

"Steph, I really thought you were going to beat Chloe out this year," she said softly. Their group was spread far enough apart that the others couldn't hear them.

"I tried," she admitted. "I mean, I know we're on the same team and all...," Stephanie let her sentence trail off.

"I understand, but it also feels like we're competing against her," she said with a nod. "Personally, I know I could never beat her, but I can sure see how frustrating it must be for someone who was almost able to beat her. I don't know if I could still be friends with her," she chuckled. "You must be a much better person than I am is all I'm saying."

Stephanie didn't respond. Yeah, she and Chloe were what most people would consider friends. They'd hung out together for forever, like going to the same sleepovers or birthday parties. And being on the same teams, you end up getting to know a person. When they were younger, the fact that Chloe always seemed a little better than everyone else hadn't really registered with Stephanie.

It wasn't until sometime in middle school that she'd started to notice it. The teachers treated Chloe a little differently, and so did the parents. And the boys. It seemed as though every single one of them tripped all over themselves trying to help her out. It was disgusting.

Chloe always laughed it off and seemed almost oblivious to it. Maybe she was, but Stephanie had a hard time believing that Chloe wasn't aware of how others treated her. It was painfully obvious to anyone around her. Stephanie didn't want to think that she was so self-absorbed she didn't even notice that nobody else got the royal treatment like Chloe did.

"Her campout party is the best, though," Abigail continued, "so, I guess it all works out. I heard there's even going to be fireworks this year." She continued to talk on and on about everything people were saying about the bonfire. It seemed everyone was really looking forward to this year's bonfire, which was probably more due to the fact that every year it seemed to get bigger and bigger, and not just because of the fireworks.

Stephanie had to admit she felt terrible for thinking badly of Chloe. How many times had she stayed at Chloe's house or gone to her bonfires? She felt two-faced about her growing feelings of animosity, but she couldn't help it. During the last student council meeting which they'd held at Chloe's house, Stephanie felt as though she would crawl out of her skin every time she heard Chloe's voice.

The only thing that had kept her from running out the door was eating a whole stack of cookies instead. If she kept that up, she'd have to start doing extra runs to stay in shape. Her weight had never been a problem before, but if she didn't stop eating to cope with her frustrations, she'd have to go on a diet.

"By the way, did you ever ask Jared out? I know you were thinking about it but hadn't decided," Abigail asked, pulling Stephanie back to the present.

"No," she confessed. "I thought about it when I was talking to him the other day, but he just kept watching Chloe the whole time. I figured why bother."

"Man, that sucks," Abigail said. "I know how much you like him."

Stephanie shrugged, but she could feel her stomach start to do flip flops just thinking about him. It had taken her forever just to admit to someone that she liked him. When she'd finally screwed up the courage to talk to him, his concentration on Chloe had been hard to take.

"Sometimes I feel like Chloe sucks the fun out of everything," Stephanie blurted out. She hadn't meant to say it out loud, but now that she had, it was like a weight had been lifted from her shoulders. After all, that was how she really felt. Even though everyone seemed to like Chloe, there had to be a few others who felt the same way she did.

Abigail burst out laughing so hard they had to stop jogging for a moment for her to catch her breath. She coughed a few times before nodding and starting to jog again.

"I guess I can see that. She's got the best grades, and everyone likes her, especially the boys. Add to that her running skills and the bonfire, and she's almost untouchable. It's kind of surprising she's not a you know what," she said censoring herself as they jogged by some children playing nearby.

"Right? It's annoying. And she's so flipping nice to everyone that you look like a jerk if you don't like her. It's as if she's cast a spell or something over everyone," Stephanie admitted. "Granted, being her friend does come with perks, but something's got to give."

"I don't think she could be any more perfect if she tried. But that's the thing, right? She's not even trying, while the rest of us are left feeling like fat ugly trolls with no brains."

This time it was Stephanie who was left laughing. "Exactly. Which is why life can be so unfair."

As they rounded the last corner, they saw the group meeting after their run. Chloe was standing there with her phone in hand, waving everyone in as they drew closer. When she saw her, Stephanie wanted to knock that brand-new cell phone in the dirt and stomp on it.

"Come here, ladies. I want to make sure to tell you this before anyone leaves." She was smiling brightly and while she was winded, she still looked much better than Stephanie felt. Even though Stephanie was used to running, today she hadn't felt up to it. She really wished she'd stayed in bed, although it was nice to hear someone else complain about Chloe.

"She must be one of those girls that doesn't sweat," Abigail said beside her. "Instead, she glistens," she joked. Both girls laughed as they came to a stop. They paced around as they slowly lowered their heart rate and waited for the rest of the team. Stephanie tried her best to ignore Chloe. If she didn't, she was sure her heart rate would never come back down.

"I told the coach we were all practicing today, and he said he was extremely proud of our initiative," Chloe said to the assembled group of girls. "He said he knows it's summer vacation, but he found out the school's going to be open the day after tomorrow for most of the day. He wanted to ask everyone who could to please come in around 8:00. The band is meeting there and so are a couple other groups, so he thought it would be easier for all of us to meet at school.

"He wants to look into fundraisers so we can get new uniforms next year. He said if you can't make it, that's fine, but if you can, he'd really appreciate it." She turned to the girl beside her and began to answer her question as Abigail scoffed beside Stephanie.

"I could make it, but I'm not going to," Abigail said. "No way am I getting up that early during summer vacation. They're just lucky I run to keep from eating all summer, otherwise I wouldn't be here either," she laughed. "And who appointed Chloe as spokesperson of the team? Now we have to listen to her, too?"

Stephanie felt the same way. The more she thought about everything, the madder she got. She'd been thinking about doing something that would knock Chloe down a peg. One night a few weeks ago, when she couldn't sleep, she'd actually made a plan. She wasn't sure if she would actually go through with it, but it helped calm her enough so that eventually she could get to sleep.

Now that she'd talked to Abigail, she wondered if maybe she should go ahead with it. At the time, she'd thought she was the only one who felt that way about Chloe. Knowing there was at least one other person who was disgusted by Chloe made her hopeful there were more.

"Man, I really wish someone would nudge her off her pedestal," Abigail muttered as they stepped away from the group. "I don't want something terrible to happen to her or anything like that, but I wouldn't mind if someone put a little dull finish on her shine, if you know what I mean."

Stephanie didn't answer. She was thinking about her plan and wondering if this might be the perfect time for it. If she and Abigail felt like they did about Chloe, there had to be others. Others who were too kind to do anything about it and just suffered in silence. Of course, if Stephanie executed her plan, nobody could know she was the one who had taken Chloe down, but she was okay with that. She just wanted the other girls to be able to feel important and step out of the long shadow that Chloe cast.

"Would you text me after the meeting if you go?" Abigail asked as she spotted her mom in the distance, waiting to pick her up.

"Sure, not a problem. I'm not sure if I'll go, but if I do, I'll let you know what happens," Stephanie agreed.

"Cool, thanks. See you later," she said waving before jogging off.

"See you," Stephanie muttered distracted by her plan. She was starting to think that maybe, just maybe, she had a job to do.

CHAPTER EIGHT

Holly was nervous at breakfast the following morning. Katie had called Grandpa the night before and explained everything. He'd said he was more than happy to meet Holly the next day and invited everyone over for a visit. Allen was staying home so he could work, and Steven was working as a part-time waiter, so he couldn't go. Holly was glad Lissa was going with her. At least she'd have a somewhat friendly face with her.

"Is it okay if I bring my backpack?" Holly asked as she finished up her pancakes. "I like to carry stuff with me all the time, if I can."

"Sure, I don't think that's a problem. It's a bit of a drive, anyway. He lives here in town, but in the opposite direction. Bringing something to keep yourself occupied is probably a good idea," Katie said as she cleaned up the kitchen. She excused herself, leaving Holly and Lissa alone.

"Are you nervous?" Lissa asked when she noticed Holly fidgeting, first with her hair, then with her shirt, and finally with her shoes. She'd tied and re-tied her shoelaces three times while they'd been sitting at the table.

"Sorry," Holly said as she dropped her foot to the ground. "Yes, a little."

"Grandpa's a good guy. Don't worry about him," she said as she shoved her last bite into her mouth. "I bet he's excited to meet you, too."

"Do you think?" Holly asked as she chewed on the corner of her thumb.

"Yes," Lissa chuckled as she pushed Holly's hand gently away from her mouth. "I'm absolutely sure, but you really need to relax. There's nothing to worry about. Come on, let's help Mom so we can get going."

A short time later, the breakfast dishes were cleared away, and the three of them were in Katie's minivan. Holly had put her small camera in her backpack as well as the notebook and a book to read on the way there. She was hoping she could get a few answers by meeting her mother's father, like why her mom felt as though everyone had abandoned her. She didn't want to bombard her grandfather with questions as soon as she got there, but if the opportunity came up, she'd definitely ask a few. Maybe he could shed some light on a few things.

Lissa sat beside her and pushed earbuds into her ears. Turning towards Holly, she said, "If you need anything, just tap me. I like to listen to my music loud, but you won't bother me if you want to talk." She smiled her big, hopeful grin and Holly nodded. She knew when Lissa hit play because the music, thin and tinny, could be heard from where she was sitting in the minivan.

Holly looked at Katie's eyes in the rearview mirror of the van. She began to wonder what her life would have been like if her mother had stayed in Springfield rather than taking off for Colorado. While it would have been amazing to grow up with cousins and family, she couldn't imagine never getting the opportunity to meet everyone back home in Cottonwood Springs, like Brigid, Linc, Jett, and her boyfriend, Wade. She missed him even though they'd been texting while she'd been gone. It just felt strange being away from all of them.

Sitting back, Holly allowed the time to pass by thinking of all her friends back home and imagining what they were doing at that moment. She hoped Brigid and Linc were having a good time on their honeymoon. Hopefully Brigid hadn't found another murder to investigate or something like that, although Holly was beginning to suspect that Brigid secretly liked doing all that sleuthing. And, Holly had to admit, it seemed she'd also been bitten by the bug.

Eventually, Katie pulled off the highway and began driving through a suburban neighborhood. Holly continued to watch the landscape, taking in the homes lining the streets and even the gas station on the corner. She silently wondered how different it must look now compared to when her mother left her home for the last time. She could almost imagine her walking down the side of the road, heading to a friend's house or going somewhere to get a bottle of soda.

Finally, they pulled into a long driveway that ended beside a sprawling one-story home. It reminded Holly of Katie's home. Well-kept and simple. It had grey siding with decorative maroon shutters. The front door opened and a grey-haired older man came shuffling out. He was slightly stooped as he walked, but he still looked healthy and sturdy, even if he was moving a bit slow.

"Well, hello," he called out. He was wearing faded jeans and a dark green flannel shirt. His large glasses had slid down to the end of his nose.

"We're here!" Katie called to him as they climbed out of her minivan. Holly pulled her backpack over her shoulders and faced her grandpa nervously. She felt butterflies fluttering in her stomach, and she hoped she wouldn't throw up. Swallowing hard, she took a deep breath and attempted to settle herself. Plastering a smile on her face, she tried to remind herself that he was her grandfather. There was no reason to be nervous.

"Well, I'll be," he said as he drew closer. "This must be my other granddaughter. Holly, is it?" he asked.

"Yes, sir," she said politely.

"Don't give me any of that 'sir' stuff. I'm your grandpa. Come here," he said as he opened his arms and pulled her in. Holly was taken completely by surprise, but responded with a hug of her own once she recovered. The old man squeezed her much tighter than she would have expected, making her smile a bit.

Once he released her, he held onto her arms and looked her up and down. "Now I want to take a good look at you." It seemed that he found her suitable and patted her on the arm. "Come on, young lady. Let's get to know each other." Then he gave Lissa a big squeeze and herded all three of them inside.

"Did you have anything you needed to do today, Katie?" he asked as they stepped into the living room. Holly looked around at the family photos that were on the walls and a tall table near the wall.

"Well, I do need to go pick up a few things, but I thought the girls and I could do that later," she said as she looked at Holly.

"Nonsense, the girls and I will be just fine. You go do whatever needs to be done. We can manage, can't we, girls?" he said turning to the two teenage girls who both nodded affirmatively.

"Well, if you insist," Katie said. "I'll be gone for a while."

"Take all the time you need," he said as he escorted her to the door. When she'd finally left, he turned and smiled. "Now that the boss is gone, we can enjoy ourselves. Who wants ice cream?"

Holly was surprised but smiled. Ice cream was one of her favorite snacks.

"I think you know the answer to that one," Lissa said with a laugh.

"You like ice cream?" he asked Holly.

"Like it? I love it. One of my favorite things to eat," she admitted.

"Mine, too," he said smiling. He shuffled by them and then turned, looking closely at her. "What's your favorite?"

"Rocky road," Holly answered quickly.

"Yep, you're my granddaughter," he said as he turned and headed for the kitchen. Holly looked around the living room one more time. The furniture was slightly dated and the walls were painted a simple white, but everything was tidy and in its place. Smiling, she turned and followed the other two into the kitchen.

Grandpa had already started pulling out three bowls and filling them with rocky road. Once he put it away, he opened a cabinet door and pulled out a bag of marshmallows and chocolate syrup.

"Lissa and I like a bit extra on ours. How about you?" he asked.

"I haven't ever added extra marshmallows before," Holly admitted.

"Then you're in for a real treat," he said as he added some to each one. After sticking spoons into the ice cream, he slid two bowls across the counter top.

Holly looked at her heaping bowl of ice cream and wondered what kind of adult fed kids ice cream before lunch. Not that she was complaining. If this was what grandpas were like, she wished she had three more.

CHAPTER NINE

Leah and Chloe had been friends since kindergarten when they sat next to each other on the first day of school. Leah had been to every birthday party, sleepover, and bonfire Chloe had ever hosted. That's why it really surprised Leah when she realized she wasn't a big fan of Chloe's anymore.

It wasn't that her friend had really done anything specifically wrong. Leah was fairly sure it had been a slow process. Small little things had built up over time and she finally realized that she really didn't care for Chloe like she had when they were growing up. She was trying to ignore the growing resentment she felt toward her longtime friend, but it was getting harder and harder.

Pacing around her room, deciding what to wear, Leah thought she knew when it had all started. When she was ten, at her fifth-grade birthday party, she'd tried to have a big party like Chloe always had. She invited all of her classmates to the park, determined to have a party just as big as Chloe's had been.

When only half of them showed up, she was crushed. To anyone else, it probably would have looked like a great birthday. For Leah, it was the worst day ever. It was then that she realized the world wasn't always fair. All she'd wanted was to feel as special on her big day as Chloe had. When it didn't happen, that was the start of her resentment.

In middle school, people started calling her Chloe's shadow. They all meant it as a joke, because Chloe was fair with her blonde hair and light eyes while Leah was darker skinned with black hair and brown eyes. Chloe and Leah were always together. As they grew older, Chloe filled out and dyed her hair even blonder, making her even more eye-catching than before.

Leah continued to walk around her small lavender colored room, trying to decide if she had the courage to ask Jayce out. She'd been wanting to ask him out for a long time, but she'd always ended up talking herself out of it.

Jayce had moved in just down the street about five years ago. He'd seen her trying to ride her skateboard up and down the sidewalk and had come over to help. They'd been friends ever since. Even on that first day, with Jayce's hand on her arm helping her to balance, she knew she liked him. That crush had grown over the years. So many times when they were playing video games or chatting through text messages she wanted to tell him how she felt. She'd type it out or picture it in her mind. She'd psych herself up time and time again only to wait too long and have the moment slip by.

Not today, though. She'd done her hair and put on just a touch of makeup. After changing her outfit a million times, she'd finally decided on a cute corduroy skirt and the top she always wore with it, a white breezy thing that felt like silk on her skin.

"Come on, Leah," she said to herself as she stopped in front of her full-length mirror. "You can do this. It's just Jayce. He's sweet and kind and so smart. There's no way he'll tease or make fun of you. But you can't have what you want if you don't reach for it. If you want to go out with him, you're going to have to ask him, since he doesn't have a clue about how you feel. Maybe he wants to ask you out, but he's afraid that you think of him only as a friend," she said, trying to convince herself.

She took a deep breath and walked over to her bedroom door. She put her hand on the knob to open it and froze. *I just have to go talk to Jayce like I've done so many other times*, she thought. She turned around and looked at her room, seeing all the clothes she'd tried on earlier scattered all over the place.

"I better pick all this up," she said aloud, postponing leaving. She told herself it wasn't because she was nervous. No. It was because her mom would freak out if she saw the mess and just might step outside and yell at her if she saw it. How embarrassing would it be to be trying to ask a guy out and have your mom yelling from the yard that you had clothes laying all over the place? Most likely she would add something about living in a pigsty or some other equally horrifying generalization.

Finally, after picking everything up, she knew it was time. There was no way she could put it off any longer. She wasn't sure if she could do it if she thought about the whole thing. Instead, she broke it down into manageable bits. *I'm just going to the front door*, she told herself at first. Then, *I'm just walking down the street*. Once she made it to his house she thought, *I'm just checking to see what he's up to.*

She rang the doorbell and waited. Leah knew both of Jayce's parents worked during the day, but he'd still be there. He was probably playing his newest game online or something. After a few moments, she heard the sound of approaching footsteps.

"Hey," Jayce said as he pulled open the door. He was so incredibly tall. Already over six feet, he towered over her. His blonde hair was longer on top and hung over his left eye. "What's up?"

"How's it going?" she asked. "Having fun playing video games all day?"

He laughed as he held the door open for her. "Yeah, something like that. Actually, I'm glad you came over."

"Oh?" Leah asked, a slight flutter of excitement running through her.

"Yeah, I wanted to ask you something," he said as he led her to the front room. He held up a bag of chips. "You want some? Or maybe a can of pop?"

"No, I'm good," she said waving the offer away. She joined him on the couch as he placed the video game on pause.

"I've been thinking a lot lately," he began. "I've had my eye on this girl for a while. She's really pretty and nice. Everyone likes her, but I don't think I have a chance with her."

Leah wiped her sweaty palms on her skirt. *Is he talking about me?* she wondered. *Could he possibly have felt the same way I feel this whole time and been too afraid to say anything?* She continued to listen nervously.

"I thought about asking some of the guys about this, but well, you know how they are," he shrugged. "Teenage guys aren't exactly who you ask when you need encouragement to ask a girl out," he muttered.

Leah laughed nervously. "I wouldn't imagine so. Especially knowing who some of those guys are."

"Right," he said, continuing, "so I started racking my brain on how to go about all of this. Finally, I decided. The answer was in front of my face the whole time, and I never even realized it. The answer, Leah, is you."

Ears buzzing, Leah felt as though her head had just become a helium filled balloon and lifted from her shoulders. She opened her mouth to speak, but he kept talking.

"Since you're her best friend, I thought I would ask you. Do you think Chloe would go to the Tripping Daisies concert with me this weekend?" he asked.

Leah snapped her mouth shut. It took her a moment to recover, considering that wasn't at all what she'd thought he was going to say. "Chloe?" she asked.

"Yeah, that's the girl I've had a crush on. I mean, I know she doesn't actually 'date' anyone, but it's just a concert, right? I mean, we could just go as friends or whatever. Just to hang out," he said as he continued to talk, but Leah tuned him out.

Chloe? she thought. He wants to take Chloe to the Tripping Daisies concert? She could see that his mouth was still moving, but he was completely oblivious to the fact she wasn't listening. *I'm the one who told him about that band. He wouldn't have known they existed if it wasn't for me!* The more she thought about it, the madder she became. Suddenly everything that Chloe had ever beaten her at came crashing down, from the fourth-grade spelling bee, to the birthday party, and now Jayce. Added to everything that had happened in between, Leah had had enough.

She stood up and rushed towards the front door.

"Hey, where are you going?" Jayce asked.

"I have to go," she said as she pulled the door open and hurried outside.

This was the final straw. Leah had playfully been thinking about ways to trip up Chloe. Little things that could happen to help her fall from grace. Now, she planned to revisit them. It was time to make perfect little Chloe not so perfect anymore.

CHAPTER TEN

"You know, I still have boxes and boxes of your mom's old stuff," Grandpa said as they were finishing up their bowls of ice cream.

"Really?" Holly said, surprised. "Why, after all these years?" It was mind-blowing to think in this house there was a room that held what used to be her mother's things. What would be in there? She felt as though this woman she was learning about was a complete stranger to her. There was nothing about her that sounded remotely like the woman who had given birth to her. Holly was struggling to put the two women together. How could a girl who had lived such a normal life turn into an addict who didn't care for her only child?

"Well, it was probably me avoiding it more than anything," he admitted as he stood up and collected the now empty bowls. "Although I don't think I could tell you what I was actually avoiding. Possibly it was my mistakes. It's much easier to pack things in a box and forget about them. Once Louise was gone, I didn't feel like doing much for a long time. That was your grandmother. I haven't changed much of anything since then if I could help it." He sighed as he set the empty bowls in the kitchen sink before making his way back to the table.

"I can understand that," Holly said. "I had a tough time going through our old trailer and picking out what I thought was important."

Lissa was listening quietly, a somber look on her face.

"If you don't mind, I think I'm going to go turn on the television and catch the weather. Why don't you and Lissa go in the back room and look through the boxes. I'd be more than happy to ship anything you'd like to have. Don't worry about the expense. I can manage," he said softly. Holly thought she could see a tear collecting in the corner of his eye.

"Are you sure?" she asked.

"Positive," he said with a smile. "You know, other than your hair color is different than your mom's, you're the spitting image of her. I'm so glad you came to visit. When you're done, we can talk more. Okay with you?"

Holly nodded, a lump forming in her throat. She swore she saw a single tear slide down the old man's cheek before he turned and made his way back to the front room.

"You ready?" Lissa asked.

"I think so," Holly replied. "But don't be surprised if I cry," she admitted as they stood up and headed towards the back of the house.

"Don't worry, I won't," Lissa said as she gently reached out and placed her hand on her cousin's back.

They quietly slipped by Grandpa as he was sitting in his recliner, watching the weather forecast. Holly and Lissa looked at the photos hanging on the walls in the hallway as they walked past them. Holly was starting to piece together who each person was. It was odd to sometimes see what almost looked like her own face staring back at her.

"This should be it," Lissa said, as she turned the knob on the door at the end of the hall.

Holly couldn't help but feel anxious as the door slowly opened. In front of her was a room that looked as though someone was moving out or moving in. A bed was taken apart and propped up against one wall. A vanity was tucked in another corner, bare except for the years of wear. Nicks and scratches had roughed it up, but it still looked solid and well loved. In the middle were boxes of various sizes. None were labeled.

"Where do you want to start?" Lissa asked as they stepped into the room.

"I guess with the closest ones," Holly shrugged. She unfolded the flaps on the nearest box and began to rifle through the contents. It looked as though someone had haphazardly put the contents of the room in the box. There was no rhyme or reason to any of it. There were CD's and a CD player, so they plugged it in and began to listen to them as they went through more boxes.

Eventually, Holly opened a box full of books. She almost closed it back up, but then she caught sight of something glittering at the bottom of the box.

"What's that?" she said, thinking aloud. Pulling out a stack of novels, she found it was a glittering diary. The cover was plastic but it looked like blue glitter. The latch was undone, as if the owner didn't care who read it.

"Is that a diary?" Lissa asked.

Holly flipped open the little book and recognized the handwriting even though it was slightly different from what she remembered.

"This is my mother's," she whispered. Running her fingers over the words, she quickly glanced at them. It seemed to be just an average day in the life of a high schooler. Talk of friends, teachers, and other everyday issues. She tucked it in her backpack and continued to search. "I'll read it later," Holly said. "I'd rather look through these boxes for now."

"That's probably smart," Lissa said nodding.

Holly emptied one box by putting some of its contents into another. Then, she began to place the items that she wanted to keep in the empty one. There wasn't much she wanted to keep, but a few things seemed to jump out at her, like some stuffed animals, figurines, a jewelry box. She and Lissa carefully packed them in the box so when it went through the mail nothing would get broken. After a while, they heard snores coming from the front room.

"Sounds like Grandpa fell asleep," Lissa giggled.

"I'd say so," Holly laughed. "That's some serious snoring."

Lissa looked at her phone. "Mom shouldn't be gone too much longer. We better hurry, so you can talk to him a little before she gets here."

Holly nodded. "Okay. Anyway, we're on the last box," she said as she grabbed the one that had been sitting all by itself in the corner. Opening it, she saw there were mostly old clothes and scarves in it, nothing of importance. "We better get back to Grandpa."

He may have been her grandfather, but she didn't really know him. It was time for her to change all that and get to know him.

Lissa and Holly put the room back together and slid the two boxes of items to be shipped beside the door. That way there would be no mistaking which ones she wanted. Holly picked up her backpack, and they headed back down the hall and sat down on the couch waiting for their grandfather to wake up.

Sensing the two girls had returned, Grandpa stopped snoring and opened his eyes. "Did you find anything you'd like to have?" he asked, sleepily.

"Thank you, yes, I did. I put two boxes next to the door that I wouldn't mind having," Holly said politely.

"Not a problem, kiddo," he said as he sat up. "Why don't you tell me about yourself?"

"What do you want to know?" Holly asked. She wasn't used to telling people who she was. Where would she even begin?

"Start by telling me where you live and all the people in your life now," he said. "I want to get to know you."

Holly felt her heart expand as she began to tell her grandfather all about Cottonwood Springs and her life there.

CHAPTER ELEVEN

"Thank you for everything," Holly said as she hugged her grandfather when they were ready to leave.

"No thanks necessary, punkin. I hope you get to visit me again before you head back home," he said.

"Me, too," she said warmly. "It's nice to have some people to call family after all this time." She turned to Katie and handed the woman her phone. "Would you take a picture of the two of us together?"

"Absolutely," Katie said smiling. She snapped the picture and handed the phone back to Holly. Are you two ready to go?"

The girls said their goodbyes and got into Katie's minivan. Soon, they were on the road heading back to the house.

"Do you think we'll figure out what happened with your mom and my mom from the diary?" Lissa whispered as she leaned towards Holly. Katie was too busy focusing on traffic and singing along with the song on the radio to notice.

"I hope so. Do you think we should ask your mom about it?" Holly asked as she watched Katie in the rearview mirror.

Lissa shook her head. "No. Let's see if we find anything out. I trust my mom and all, but she's been acting evasive whenever your mother's name comes up. It's like she's trying to hide something. I don't want her to know we have the diary yet, just in case."

Holly nodded. "You may be right. As soon as we can, let's start reading it."

Lissa sat back up and pushed her earbuds in her ears, leaving Holly to her thoughts on the rest of the ride back home.

When they got home, Holly and Lissa were heading up the stairs when they heard Steven's voice in the other room.

"What?" he exclaimed.

Both girls turned to each other and Lissa shrugged. Steven appeared in the doorway.

"What's wrong?" Lissa asked. Katie was setting her purse down on the end table by the front door, and she turned to listen as well.

"Chloe just sent out a mass text saying the bonfire has been cancelled until further notice," he said disappointedly.

"Why?" Katie asked. "Did something happen?"

"I don't know," Steven said, his focus still on his phone. "I'm sending her a message now to ask what's going on."

"Well, if they just need help or something, I can do it. I know how important it is to everyone," Katie said as she walked towards the living room.

"How was Grandpa's?" Steven asked as he waited for a reply from Chloe.

"It was good," Holly said.

"She and Grandpa really hit it off," Lissa explained.

"Well, he's a pretty laid-back guy," Steven said smirking. His phone buzzed and he looked down at it. "What?" he asked, sounding shocked.

"What is it?" Lissa asked.

"Chloe said the school is accusing her of vandalism. Her parents are livid and didn't believe her when she told them she didn't do it," he answered as he typed. "I'm asking her what she supposedly did."

They all waited at the bottom of the stairs for the reply.

"She says someone wrote swear words and stuff all over the lockers at school with dry erase markers. The school said it won't press charges if she comes in and cleans everything off the lockers. I guess there's a security video of someone who looks just like her doing it. Bad thing is, she was home alone when it happened, and she doesn't have any way to prove that it wasn't her." Steven sighed. "I can't believe this."

"Are you sure she's telling the truth?" Holly asked.

"Oh, yeah," Lissa scoffed. "Trust me, this girl's no liar." When Holly looked confused, Lissa continued. "She's like this brainiac good girl who's also pretty and popular. Kind of like you, from what I understand."

Holly laughed, "Don't think so. I'm not popular."

"Still," Lissa continued. "She's kind of almost too perfect to be real, but she's super nice. There's no way she would do something like that. Someone had to set her up."

"But why would anyone do that?" Steven asked. "I thought everybody loved the bonfires. She invites, like, everyone. Whoever did this just ruined the fun for everyone."

"What if she proves she didn't do it?" Holly asked.

"I would assume the bonfire would be back on," Steven said. "But how could she do that when she doesn't have anybody who can verify that she was at home?"

"Simple," Holly shrugged. "Find out who really did it."

"But how?" Lissa asked. "We're just kids, not the cops."

"Which is even better. Remember how I told you Brigid's helped with lots of police investigations? That's because people are much more comfortable talking to people just like them. They'll watch what they say and not tell the police everything they know because they're afraid they might incriminate themselves or rat out a friend or relative. But a couple of teenagers asking questions?" Holly asked. She knew she already had her hands full trying to figure out what happened with her mother, but she was sure she could help find out who had vandalized the school lockers.

She couldn't let someone be accused of something they didn't do, especially one of her cousins' friends. Besides, it seemed like this bonfire was important to a lot of people, and it looked like it was up to her to try and make it happen as planned.

"Can you help, Holly?" Steven asked. "I know it's not really your problem, but I consider Chloe a good friend."

"Not a problem," Holly said. "We should probably plan this out somewhere a little more comfortable, though," she said looking around the entry.

"Oh, right," Steven said. "Come on, let's go up to my room."

They jogged up the stairs and headed down the hall. Holly dropped her backpack by her door as they walked by the guest room.

When Holly went into Steven's room, she felt like she'd walked into a different house. While the rest of the house was decorated in light, airy colors, Steven's room was dark blue. The walls were nearly bare with the exception of a framed poster above his bed from some old horror movie. Piles of dirty clothes were in the corner beside a desk that had a reading lamp on.

Steven pulled out the desk chair for Holly, and he and Lissa sat on his bed. "Where would we even start?" he asked.

"Typically, you need to start with a list of suspects," Holly began. "Anyone who has any reason for vandalizing the lockers. Does Chloe have anyone who doesn't like her?"

"Honestly, I don't think so," Steven explained. "I mean, she's nice to everyone."

"Yeah, but that doesn't mean anything," Lissa pointed out. "Girls can be sweet to your face while they stab you in the back."

"Lissa's got a point," Holly said. "We'll probably have to ask Chloe if she knows anyone who might have had a reason to do it. It wouldn't hurt if we could take a look at the video footage, too. That might give us some clues." She tapped her chin as she began to think.

"What should we do once we have a list of suspects?" Lissa asked.

"Typically, you go down the list and see who was doing what at the time it happened. If they don't have an alibi, you dig further. Ask questions and things like that until you narrow it down," Holly explained.

"That seems almost too easy," Steven said skeptically.

"It may sound simple, but trust me, it's not," Holly assured them. "Sometimes people lie or give you half the truth. Other times, it may seem like one person is the offender, but then you find out it's someone else."

"We need to talk to Chloe," Steven said.

"That should be your first step," Holly agreed.

Steven pulled out his phone and began furiously typing. "I'm telling her we want to help clear her name and for her to ask her parents if we can come over and talk to her sometime soon," he said.

Lissa and Holly waited for him to get a response. When he finally did, they listened anxiously as he read it.

"She says her parents don't mind if we come over after a while," he said as he typed his response.

"Where does she live?" Holly asked.

"Just the next street over," Lissa answered. "Most of the kids who go to our high school live fairly close by."

"That's handy," Holly remarked.

"When shall I tell her we'll be at her house?" Steven asked.

Holly thought about the diary tucked safely in her backpack. What she really wanted to do was go to her room and read through it. She'd only be in Springfield for a short time, and she didn't want to miss an opportunity to find out why her mom had moved away. Yet looking at her cousins, she knew she couldn't say no to them. Their friend needed help, and if Holly was in her shoes, she hoped someone would be willing to help her.

"I guess the sooner the better," she said.

CHAPTER TWELVE

They told Katie they were going over to Chloe's house and then they began the short walk around the block. Holly brought the notebook they were using to investigate their family, so they could also record anything they needed to remember about Chloe's situation.

While they walked, Lissa and Steven told Holly about some of their favorite places in Springfield. Lissa couldn't talk enough about the nature museum, while Steven told her about his favorite hangout spots. Eventually, they turned and walked up a long sidewalk to a large white two-story home. Holly thought the house looked like something she'd see in a magazine or on television. There was even a summer-themed wreath on the front door.

As they were walking up the steps to the house, a girl about Steven's age opened the door. Her long platinum blonde hair shone brightly in the sunlight. Her nose was pink and her eyes were red-rimmed, as though she'd been crying.

"Thank you so much for coming over," she said to Steven as she hugged him.

"Hey, no problem, Chloe. I just can't believe someone would do this," he said, returning the embrace.

"I know," she said, a single tear slipping down her cheek. "Please come inside."

"Chloe, this is Holly. She's our cousin from Colorado, and she's going to help us investigate this whole thing," Steven said. "Actually, it was her idea. She's investigated things like this before."

"I really appreciate it. Thanks," Chloe said as she pulled Holly in for a hug. Holly felt awkward hugging a stranger, but she tried not to let it show.

"I'll do my best," Holly said, "but I can't make any promises."

"I'm sure it will be better than anything I could do. Let's go sit in the dining room. My parents are watching their game shows in the family room," she said, rolling her eyes.

The house was large and spacious. The tall ceilings and hardwood floors told Holly the home was old, her favorite kind of a house. She thought older houses had a lot more character and detail than the newer ones.

Chloe pushed a set of wooden double doors open and they walked into a room with a fairly large dining room table which could easily seat eight people.

"Do you guys want anything to drink or snack on?" she asked.
"No, I think we're good," Steven said looking at his sister and Holly who nodded in agreement.

"So, where do we start?" Chloe asked as they all sat down at the table.

"First of all, we need to come up with a list of suspects," Holly explained. She opened the notebook to a fresh sheet of paper. "Do you know anyone who would want to see you get in trouble?"

"No. That's the thing," Chloe said, almost whining. "I always try to be nice and kind to everyone. I don't know who would want to do something like this to me." She looked as though she wanted to burst into tears.

"Take a deep breath," Holly said easily. It was a good thing she'd read all those books on psychology a year or two ago. She had a feeling she may need to use some of the things she'd read about. She waited for Chloe to collect herself before continuing. "Steven said there was some film from a security camera at the school."

"Yes," Chloe said as she pulled her phone out of her pocket. "They emailed it to my parents to show them it was me." She tapped a few times on her phone and then slid it over to them. Lissa pushed play as they all huddled around the phone.

A young lady wearing a zip-up hoodie was scrawling obscenities and drawing vulgar things on the school lockers. Her face was obscured, but there was a bit of light blonde hair peeking out from under the hoodie as she moved from locker to locker. Suddenly, the girl froze and then bolted toward the stairs. A pudgy janitor followed her, but she was too fast for him.

"Chloe, that does look a lot like you," Steven said.

"I know, but here's the thing. That's my hoodie, the one my grandmother made me, but its been missing. It's not in my closet," Chloe said as she leaned across the table, retrieving her phone.

"What do you mean?" asked Lissa. "Everyone knows that's your jacket."

"Which is exactly what whoever did it wanted people to think when they saw the camera footage," Holly filled in. Everyone turned and looked at her. "Well, think about it. If you want to frame someone, what's the best way to do it?"

They were quiet until Steven said, "Make it look like they did it."

"Exactly. If a person is known for wearing something, why not wear it while committing the crime? They're taking advantage of the fact that when people see that jacket, they'll automatically think of you. I'm willing to bet your hair is fairly unique, too," Holly suggested.

"You're right. No one else has hair this light," Chloe admitted.

Holly nodded. "So now we need to figure out who could have taken your jacket," she said. "Any ideas where to start? When did it go missing?"

"Well, I know I still had it when school let out for summer vacation," she began. "I had some of the cross country girls over maybe a week ago. I think I noticed it missing a day or two later. I mean, it's not exactly the right time of year to wear a jacket," she pointed out.

"No, that's for sure," Holly agreed. "Has anyone else come over to your house from the time school ended until you realized it was missing?" she asked.

Chloe shook her head. "I don't think so."

"Hey, how's it going?" a deep voice asked. They all turned to see a teenage boy entering the dining room.

"Hey, Seth," Chloe said. "Holly, this is my younger brother Seth. He's a junior."

"Nice to meet you, Holly," Seth said. His dark hair was short but slightly shaggy. His eyes were a bright green and took her by surprise. He had a cocky smirk that said he knew he was good looking. Holly wasn't impressed. Not that she didn't agree, but his cockiness wasn't exactly appealing to her.

"Nice to meet you," she said, turning back to Chloe. "Who all was over that day?"

Seth strolled over to the chair beside his sister and sat down. He folded his fingers as he listened intently.

"Hmmm," Chloe said as she began to think. "I'm pretty sure only four of them showed up. It was kind of a last-minute thing. We wanted to get a gift for our coach, and we were trying to figure out what to buy him."

Holly nodded. "Four is good. I was afraid you were going to say something around ten or so," she said with a nervous laugh.

"What are you guys doing?" Seth asked.

"They're going to help me clear my name so we can have the bonfire," she said confidently.

"I'm going to try," Holly added, "but certainly no guarantee of success."

"She's got this. The lady she lives with solves murder investigations and stuff all the time," Lissa said. Holly could feel heat rising up in her cheeks.

"Is that so?" Seth said, eyeing Holly appreciatively. "I like a girl with brains."

Holly ignored him. "What are their names?" she asked Chloe.

"Stephanie, Allison, Leah, and Carrie," she said. "Steven and Lissa know who they are."

Steven nodded. "And thankfully, all but one of them lives somewhat nearby. So it won't be a problem to pay them a visit," he said.

"Good," Holly said nodding as she took down notes. She needed to remember the jacket, names, and the blonde hair. "None of them has blonde hair though, right?" she asked.

Chloe shook her head. "No, and the video showed someone with almost white blonde hair like mine."

"What if it was a wig?" Seth suggested.

"That's what I was just thinking," said Holly. "I would imagine it wouldn't be too hard to find one."

Seth nodded. "And fairly easy to tell who the culprit is," he said. Standing up quickly he continued. "Well, it looks like you're in good hands, Chloe. I'll leave you to it." He turned to the others. "Steven, Lissa, good to see you again. And Holly?" he said looking directly at her. "I hope to see you again, soon." He winked before turning and leaving the room.

"Ugh, brothers," Chloe scoffed.

"Hey, we aren't all bad," Steven said, mockingly acting as though he was offended.

"Maybe the sister should be the one to say that," Lissa said as she raised her eyebrows and gave him a sideways look. Chloe and Holly laughed.

"Well, the first thing we need to do is find out where these people were when the vandalism occurred," Holly pointed out. "But I think your brother is right. We should keep our eyes open for your jacket and a wig that looks similar to your hair."

"Whatever you say," Chloe said with a sigh. "I just hope we can save the bonfire."

"Me, too," Steven said. "Everybody looks forward to it all year and it's so much fun. It's kind of a highlight of the year," he said clearing his throat. Holly watched him and was pretty sure he had a crush on Chloe.

"We'll figure it out," Holly said. "It's just a matter of covering all the bases."

CHAPTER THIRTEEN

"Since it's on our way, why don't we stop and talk to Stephanie?" Lissa asked as they walked down the street. The sun was starting to sink lower in the sky, but they still had plenty of daylight left.

"Good idea, Lissa," Steven said thoughtfully. "You up for a little detour, Holly?"

"Sure, where does she live?" Holly asked as they began to take a shortcut between two houses.

"Just over that way and up one street," Steven pointed. "It won't take very long at all. The others will probably have to wait until tomorrow, though."

"Might as well see what we can find out," Holly shrugged. "Time is of the essence. The quicker we can figure out who did it, the sooner we can clear Chloe's name and save the bonfire."

Steven nodded and led them on a shortcut to Stephanie's house. Soon they were walking up a stone pathway that led to the front door. The house wasn't particularly fancy, just a single-story home with a few bushes planted along the front. After he'd knocked on the door, Steven turned around and looked at his sister and cousin.

"This is probably a waste of time. Stephanie and Chloe have been friends for forever. I can't imagine she'd do anything to hurt her," he said softly.

"Steven, trust me. You just never know what a person is capable of," Holly said just before the door was opened by a girl about their age.

"Steven, Lissa, what are you guys doing here?" she asked.

"Hey, Stephanie. I'm sure you've heard about Chloe's parents cancelling the bonfire," Steven began. "We're trying to change that and thought maybe you could help us."

"Yeah, I heard about it," she said stepping to the side and gesturing to them, "Come in." They stepped inside as Stephanie closed the door behind them.

"This is our cousin, Holly," Lissa said politely. "She's visiting from Colorado and is helping us figure out what happened."

Stephanie and Holly said hello to each other before Stephanie led them through the house. They ended up in a living room with two couches facing each other in front of a fireplace. Tall bookshelves lined one wall.

"We'll have to stay in here. My little brother's sleeping, and I don't want to wake him," she said softly.

"We won't take long," Holly assured her. "We just have a few questions we'd like to ask you. To start with, can you tell us where you were this morning?"

Stephanie looked taken aback. She shook her head to collect herself and began to speak. "I- I was here all morning. I watch my little brother during the day when I'm on summer break while my parents are to work. I've been here all day. Why?"

"Apparently someone looking like Chloe vandalized the high school this morning," Steven said as he leaned back against the couch.

"How do you know she didn't do it?" Stephanie asked. "Why are you coming over here and accusing me of doing it?" Her voice had become very shrill.

"No one is accusing you of anything," Holly said calmly. "Chloe swears she didn't do it, but she doesn't have an alibi. We're just trying to determine who may have had a motive to make it look as though Chloe did it. Someone went to a lot of trouble to make it look like Chloe did it. If they were capable of doing this to her, they could do it to anyone."

Stephanie bit her lip. "Look, I know a ton of people like Chloe, but not everyone really does," she admitted.

"What do you mean?" Lissa asked, leaning forward.

"Well, think about it," Stephanie began. "She's always number one, no matter what it is. Everyone else has to live pretty much in her shadow. There's no way for anyone to shine when she's around," she muttered.

Holly was starting to wonder if there was more going on here than she realized. Stephanie seemed extremely bitter considering she was supposed to be her friend.

"Forgive me," Holly began. "But I thought you and Chloe were friends?"

"Well, I mean, we are," Stephanie stammered. "It's just, sometimes I get tired of her getting all the attention, you know? It's as if everyone thinks Chloe can do no wrong. Everybody treats her like she's something special because of that bonfire. I mean, don't get me wrong, I like going to it. It's fun and everyone goes. But it still totally sucks to live in her shadow," she grumbled.

"How old is your little brother?" Holly asked. It wouldn't be hard for Stephanie to claim she'd been watching him and really have been doing something else. If her brother was her alibi, Holly needed to know if the boy was old enough to vouch for her.

"He's five," she said smiling. "I know older sisters aren't supposed to like their younger siblings, but I can't help it. We played video games almost all morning until lunch."

Holly nodded as she made a mental note. Stephanie could be crossed off. "Sounds like you guys had a lot of fun. Do you have any idea who may have wanted Chloe to get in trouble?"

She shook her head. "Not really. I know a few of us on the cross country team were complaining about her recently. Some of us are hoping to impress scouts from colleges so we can get scholarships. When the scouts first started showing up at our meets, we'd all get excited. Especially when we could tell who they were. You know, big name colleges and things like that.

"But then we noticed they mainly wanted to talk to her. At least the good ones. She's the star of the team, and with her around, everyone else looks dim by comparison."

Holly thought about what Stephanie had just said. She understood where Stephanie was coming from, but that didn't make it right. Was it possible that the bonfire being cancelled was just collateral damage? What if the culprit thought they could get Chloe kicked off the cross country team with the vandalism? It wasn't that far of a stretch, and since all of the suspects were on the cross country team, it was something to think about. It might simply be a coincidence, or it could be a vital clue.

"Steffy?" a tiny voice said from nearby.

Everyone turned to see a young boy leaning in the doorway, rubbing his eyes.

"What's up, Dylan?" Stephanie asked as she stood up and walked over to him.

"I'm really thirsty," he grumbled.

"Okay, just hang tight," she said. She turned back to the group and said, "I have to get him a glass of water. I'll be right back." She hurried into the other room. Meanwhile, Dylan came into the room and sat down where she'd been sitting

"What are you guys doing?" he asked.

"Just talking to your sister about a few things," Steven said smiling to the little guy. "What are you doing out of bed?"

"I woke up and needed to go to the bathroom. When I was done, I decided I was thirsty," the little boy said. "And I'm still too short to reach the cups."

"Don't worry, you'll grow," Steven reassured him.

"I hope so," Dylan said. "I'm tired of always being the short one."

"Hey, Dylan? Did you and your sister have fun this morning?" Holly asked. She didn't have any reason to think Stephanie was lying, but since the opportunity had presented itself, she might as well check her alibi.

The little boy's eyes lit up. "Yeah! We played racing games all morning. It was so much fun," he said with a grin.

Stephanie returned with a glass of ice water a few moments later.

"Here you go, bud. Now go back to bed," she said as she lightly touched his shoulder. He nodded and waved as he took a big drink and wandered off. They waited for him to get out of hearing range before they continued.

"Well, I hope you find whoever did it," Stephanie sighed. "I was really looking forward to the bonfire this year. It must be upsetting to Chloe for someone to make it look like she did this. She's got to be going out of her mind. I remember when we were in first grade and the teacher thought she'd stolen an eraser out of some other kid's desk. She cried even after the teacher apologized."

"She's not quite that worked up, but she's pretty upset," Steven said. "And she has plenty of reason to be that way. I can't imagine how betrayed she must feel right now." It looked like he was staring a hole through Stephanie, but she seemed oblivious.

"Well, thanks for taking the time to talk to us," Holly said, doing her best to wrap things up. She had a feeling Steven wasn't very happy with Stephanie. "If I have any more questions, I'll let you know." They all stood up and began to walk towards the front door.

"Sure, yeah. Let me know if you find out who did it," she said. "I'll keep my ears open in case I hear anything."

"If you do, let us know," Steven said pointedly. They stepped out the front door and into the cool early evening air.

"Well, it looks like that's one person we can mark off the list," Lissa said brightly.

"Yeah, but it may have opened up a whole new can of worms," Holly said as they started walking along the sidewalk.

CHAPTER FOURTEEN

"Mom wants us to head home," Steven said after checking his phone. He sighed and sent a reply before tucking it back in his pocket. "I can't believe so many people don't like Chloe."

They were walking in the direction of their home when Holly said, "You know, sometimes people are just ignorant. They see someone who's better than them at something and rather than just trying harder or accepting that maybe someone else is just more talented, they become envious. Envy can turn people into monsters if they let it."

She may not have been very old, but Holly had seen it plenty of times already. It didn't help her make friends when she was naturally good at learning. Other kids her age would insult her when she did better on a test or something like that, but what was she supposed to do? Not try, because they didn't learn as fast as she did?

"I know," Steven said as he kicked a pebble on the sidewalk. It made soft little crackling noises as it skipped over the cracked concrete. "It just sucks that someone would do this to Chloe. I've never seen her do a mean thing to anyone. She always tries to help anyone who asks and like I said, she invites literally everyone to her annual bonfire. I mean, who does that?" he scoffed.

"Doesn't hurt you've had a major crush on her for forever," Lissa teased.

"Shut your face," Steven said over his shoulder to his sister, but Holly could tell he wasn't angry with her. She smiled as she turned and saw Lissa stick her tongue out at her older brother behind his back. It may have been something simple, but that little exchange made Holly wish she had a sister or brother, someone to tease and bicker with as well as take care of and spend time together.

"I'm sorry you got wrapped up in all of this," Lissa said after they walked in silence for a little while. They were just a few houses down from theirs.

"It's totally fine. Don't even think about it," Holly said with a smile.

"Yeah, but you didn't come here to help someone you don't even know," Lissa sighed.

"No, I didn't," Holly conceded. "But I did come here to get to know my family. To find out where I came from and all of that good stuff. The way I see it, helping your friend is helping me get to know you guys. Gives us something to do so we don't have to have weird awkward silences."

They turned and began to walk up the driveway to their house. "Do you think we can really find out who did this?" Steven asked.

"I do," Holly said confidently. "We're going to need to do some hard work, but I absolutely believe we'll figure it out eventually."

Steven smiled as he held the door open for his sister and cousin, "I hope you're right."

"Hey, guys," Katie said cheerfully when they entered the house. "What have you been up to?"

"I think you know that someone framed Chloe by making it look like she vandalized the school. Holly's going to help us prove that she didn't do it," Lissa said brightly as they all entered.

"Is that so?" Katie asked eyeing each of them. "I hope you're being careful."

"What do you mean?" asked Steven. "It's not like we're searching for a murderer or something crazy like that. This is just some jealous high school thing that went too far."

"That may be so," Katie said putting her hands on her hips. "But you need to make sure you know the full story before you start pointing fingers at someone. There are always two sides to every story. Don't ever forget that. If you only listen to one side, you only get half the story."

"Okay," Steven and Lissa both said almost in unison. Holly watched as they excused themselves and headed upstairs. Once they were gone, she turned to her aunt.

"Aunt Katie?" she said.

"Yes, Holly?" Katie had been watching her children as they went upstairs. She turned towards Holly.

"Were you and my mom close? Like Steven and Lissa?" Holly asked. It had been on her mind since she'd spent time with her cousins. What had her mom and aunt's relationship been like? She wished she could have asked her mother, but instead her aunt would have to do.

"I think so," she said smiling warmly. "We did a lot together when we were younger."

"So what happened?" Holly pressed. "Why is it that, if you were so close, you never came to visit? You never helped my mom?" She could feel the tears that wanted to go along with those questions threatening to fall. What she really wanted to ask was *Why didn't you help me? Why did you let me live like that? Alone, scared, and with no one to help me.*

"Like I said before, there's always more than one side to every story, Holly. I'm not sure if I could even explain." Katie began looking around the room, anywhere but at Holly. The questions obviously made her uncomfortable, but at least for the moment, she wasn't shutting down.

Katie crossed her arms, sighed, and looked at Holly. "Your mother changed when she left," Katie began. "It didn't take long before I felt like I didn't even know who she was anymore. Maggie started making stupid decisions and...," she stopped herself with a sigh. "We shouldn't speak ill of the dead. Your mother made decisions I didn't agree with. We drifted apart. It's as simple as that," she said definitively.

Holly searched her aunt's face for something, anything to explain what she had been going to say before she caught herself.

Katie smiled faintly. "I better go finish up in the kitchen," she said quickly before disappearing.

Holly was left standing in the entry, wondering exactly what Katie meant. As she shuffled up the stairs, she tried to piece together what she'd figured out so far. Katie said her mother had changed and was making decisions she didn't agree with. Did it have something to do with how they ended up in Colorado?

What would make her mother pack up everything and move a whole state away from her family? Not to mention have a child, live in poverty, and become addicted to drugs and alcohol. The way her mother had always been so against speaking about her family... it reminded Holly a lot of how Katie was acting now.

The way Katie acted was almost an indication that whatever hurt her mother had felt from her family, Katie had also felt from her sister. Both seemed to feel as though the other had wronged them in some way. She remembered the diary she'd found at her grandfather's house and wondered if there were clues in any of its pages. Like it or not, the answers were here in Missouri, and she only had so much time to figure it all out. It seemed that although Katie didn't offer up any information, she would answer direct questions.

Holly thought about it and realized what she needed to do. Rather than trying to pry the entire story from Katie, she needed to ask the right questions. Maybe then, Holly could at least learn what happened from Katie's perspective. Her words were still echoing in Holly's mind about two sides to every story. Was she telling Holly she wanted Holly to see her side of what had happened?

CHAPTER FIFTEEN

After dinner Holly changed into her favorite dinosaur pajama pants and a clean Green Day shirt, grabbed her mother's diary, and climbed on the bed. She wasn't ready for sleep yet, but it felt good lounging around like she would at home. She'd stopped in the kitchen on her way to her room and grabbed a bag of chips and a can of pop for fortification, not knowing what secrets the diary might hold.

She opened the diary and tried to encourage herself to read, but after several minutes, she had to admit she was nervous. What would she find in it? Deep dark secrets or just the ramblings of a teenage girl? It was always possible her mother never wrote anything important and there would be nothing in it that would help her discover what she wanted to know.

But if I don't read it, I'll never know, she thought. Taking a deep breath, she took the hair tie from her wrist, and pulled her hair back in a messy bun. She pulled back the covers, got into bed, and started to read.

The first few entries weren't all that interesting. Her mother had written about her grades and various classes. Girls that were mean and boys in general. Nothing she read was shocking other than she discovered that her mother had gotten good grades. Great ones, actually.

"So that's where I get it from," Holly said to the empty room. In a way, she was imagining that Brigid or her sister, Fiona, was there, listening and offering support as she read. It helped her feel like she wasn't terribly alone. Not that she felt that anyone here didn't welcome her fully, it was just with the secrets her aunt was hiding, it was hard for her to feel completely comfortable. She trusted her cousins, but she still wasn't sure about the adults. She hadn't been around Allen all that much and wondered if he even knew the whole story.

Skimming through the next few pages, Holly began to look for something a little more interesting. It wasn't that she didn't want to read all of her mother's diary, it was just that while she was in Springfield, she wanted to find out why her mother had left the city and her family. The diary was somewhat thick, and she didn't want to waste time while she was in Springfield on the parts that didn't have relevant clues.

Reading on, her mother seemed to have a large group of friends, and it seemed as though she may have been one of the more popular girls in her class. Holly slowed down and began to really pay attention to what she was reading. She was trying to fit the pieces together and get a mental image of what her mother had been like when she was younger.

She imagined her mother had looked a lot like she did, since Aunt Katie had mentioned the strong resemblance and so had her grandfather. She tried to picture Maggie as if she was a character in a book, and she was reading about her. She was routinely reading along when she found one day in the diary that made her sit up. In it, her mother mentioned that she'd met a boy.

I met someone today, although I don't know if I should even write about him. He's tall, handsome, and has beautiful golden blonde hair that shimmers in the sunlight. Even on the cold winter day that I met him, he looked like a ray of sunshine. I don't want to go into too much yet, because I'm not sure if Katie has been reading my diary.

I'm going to have to hold off until I know for sure if my hiding spot is safe.

She's always nosing around in my room wanting to know what I've been doing. I don't want her opening her mouth and ruining a good thing.

Do you know how when you meet someone amazing, it seems like the world stands still? Even just the slightest touch from them can make you feel as though you've been charged with electricity. That's how I feel right now. As if I've been running around with only half the life I was supposed to have and now... now I'm fully charged.

It's as if for the first time I can see how great everything can be. Oh, how I want to say more, but I just can't. Once I know my hiding place is safe, maybe I'll write more. I need to. I don't know how much longer I can keep it all in, but for now, I have to.

"I wonder who it was," Holly said aloud to herself before she took a drink of her soda. She leaned over the side of the bed and picked up the notebook she'd been writing things down in about her mother. She flipped it open to a fresh page and wrote, "Beautiful mystery guy?" and below that she wrote "tall, blonde hair" before tossing it back down on the floor.

It might end up being nothing, but maybe not. Her instincts told her this guy wasn't just some random person that her mother never heard from again. No, he might be the clue she'd been looking for. Better to write it down and not need it, than to not write it down and waste time trying to find it later.

Her feet started to tingle, letting her know she'd been curled up on the bed for too long. Holly stood up and headed over to the window, pushing the curtains back. She had no way of knowing what direction she was facing, but she imagined she was facing home. She thought about Wade, her boyfriend back home, and all of her friends in Cottonwood Springs.

Brigid and Linc weren't there, because they were on their honeymoon, but Fiona and her husband, Brandon, along with Missy, and everyone else were. She was having a good time in Missouri, but with everything that was happening, she couldn't help but be a little homesick for Cottonwood Springs. She wished she'd brought someone with her, then maybe she wouldn't feel so out of place.

She looked at the clock and wondered if it was too late to call Wade. He was always there for her when she needed to talk. Day or night, it seemed like he always had time to listen.

Before her mom had died, they'd spoken in passing at school, but Holly never had a clue that he'd even noticed her. He was the most popular kid in their grade, athletic, and easygoing, the opposite of how Holly thought she was. But when he'd asked her to tutor him, things began to change. They'd been a couple for a while now, and Holly couldn't be happier.

She went over to her phone and sent him a quick tex. Nothing long or drawn out just, *Hey, what are you doing?*

It wasn't long before she got a response. *Nothing. I was just thinking about you, actually.*

Holly couldn't help but smile. It was great having Wade in her life. He kept her sane when school stuff sometimes got crazy. She knew she could always talk to Brigid, but she was much older than Holly. Wade was like her calm place in a storm. If she had a bad dream about her mom or just needed to vent to get things off her chest, he was the one she turned to.

Hope it was good, she replied as she smiled.

Of course it was, he replied. *How's Missouri?*

Pretty much like Colorado. Just with less people I know, she typed back.

Try to give them a chance, he responded. *I'd call you, but my parents just went to bed, and they'd probably hear me talking.*

That's okay, I understand, she said.

Still, I wish I could hear your voice. You don't have any boyfriends in Missouri yet, do you? He sent along an emoji that looked like it was scratching its chin.

Holly smiled and thought about Chloe's brother. He definitely wasn't her type, but he was obviously interested. She decided she wouldn't tell Wade about him. No reason to.

Then he texted, *But seriously, everything okay?*

Holly began to type "sure" but then she erased it. She made it a point to never lie to him, and she wasn't sure if she felt everything was okay. She was feeling small in a big world, and these two mysteries seemed way out of her league.

Just trying to figure out what made my mom not want to be around these people anymore. It's all a little much, you know? she texted back.

He took a moment to respond, but when he did, she knew she'd made the right choice in texting him.

They're just new people, and I know how you are about new people, he wrote. *Give them all and your mom the benefit of the doubt. People change. Maybe they aren't the same people your mom grew up with?*

Holly thought about that and then sent, *You're right. As usual. What would I do without you?*

Who knows? He replied.

They texted a little longer before she told him she was heading to bed. She knew she needed some sleep. Morning would come quickly, and she wanted to concentrate on finding out who was framing Chloe. She needed a good night's sleep so she could think clearly.

She charged her phone, slipped a bookmark into her mother's diary to save her space, and tossed back the covers. With her heart feeling a bit lighter after chatting with Wade, she closed her eyes and drifted off to sleep.

CHAPTER SIXTEEN

The next morning Holly woke up earlier than usual. She'd been dreaming of her mother and home before it morphed into her being in Missouri and being stuck there. No matter what she tried, she couldn't seem to get back home to Cottonwood Springs. She tossed and turned, trying to get some rest, before finally getting out of bed.

She quietly opened the door to her room, having decided to see what she could find in the kitchen for a snack. Her stomach was growling so loudly as she crept down the hall toward the stairs, she was sure she'd end up waking everyone in the house.

After finding some cereal, she hurried back to her room, and slipped back under the covers. She saw the diary she'd been reading the night before, and it called to her. She shoveled a spoonful of cereal into her mouth, and then began to wonder if the whole thing was just a waste of time. Although the diary had mentioned a guy her mother had met, that didn't mean she'd written anything else about him. Since she'd expressed concerns that Katie had been reading her diary, it was possible she never wrote anything substantial in the diary.

"I don't know if this is even worth the trouble," Holly said aloud, but even so, she found herself reaching for the diary. Her hand slid over it, and she felt a chill on her hand. Would her mother even want her reading this? Even so, her hands opened it where she'd left off the night before, and she parted the pages. It was as if they had a mind of their own. Deciding she should go with her instincts, she began to read.

There wasn't much at first, just more of the same about school and friends plus the gossip that went along with it all. But then, something caught Holly's eye.

February 20th

I don't think Katie has been reading this, and I just have to get all of this out. I haven't told anyone and having this big of a secret makes me want to explode. Remember the guy I said I'd met? I'd been standing in front of a bulletin board just inside the library, looking at a flyer for an upcoming cooking class. I've always dreamed of being a chef, so it sounded like fun. It promised to teach more than just the basics, and I could afford it with the money I'd been given for Christmas.

While I was standing there, deciding if I wanted to spend the rest of my money on this class, a guy walked up and started talking to me. This is the guy I wrote about before. He's tall, super cute, and definitely older, like 23 or 24. We got to talking, and he asked if I was going to take the class. I said I was thinking about it, but I wasn't sure. He told me he really hoped I would because then we could get to know each other a little more. I was on cloud nine! I'm sure he doesn't realize how young I am, but who cares? He didn't ask, so it must not be too important to him. I signed up for the class.

Last night was the first class, and we partnered up. He was a complete gentleman, and asked me if we could go out sometime. He wanted my phone number, but I lied and told him I didn't have one right now. There was no way I'd give him my home number and run the risk of my sister or parents answering the phone. I know I probably shouldn't be lying to him about my age, but I really like him. It's not like I'm a child. Besides, I know what I want and I won't let anything get in my way. I'm really drawn to him. Oh, and by the way, his name is Charlie.

Holly stopped reading and grabbed the notebook she'd written in the night before. Next to her notes she wrote the name "Charlie" and sat back against the headboard. As she finished her cereal and set the bowl on the night stand, her imagination began to take flight. There were so many things that could go wrong in this scenario. Did he find out how young her mother was? Did he get in trouble because the police got involved? There were so many possibilities. Holly knew the only way to find out for certain was to keep reading.

Just as she was picking up the diary again, her phone vibrated. She looked at the screen and saw that it was a message from Brigid.

How are things going there? she asked.

Holly smiled, knowing that even on her honeymoon, Brigid couldn't resist checking in. Holly had told her to not worry about messaging her, but she had to admit she was glad Brigid hadn't paid any attention to her. Right now, she felt as though she could use Brigid's calm reassurance.

Okay, I guess, Holly replied. *Getting a little homesick.*

It's tough being away from home, but enjoy it. You'll be back to your room and life before you know it, and you'll wonder what you were in such a hurry for, Brigid answered.

Holly knew she was probably right, but it still didn't make things any easier. *How's the honeymoon going?* she asked, changing the subject.

We're having a wonderful time, Brigid typed. *We're going to go lay on the beach today and just soak up the sun. I'll email you some pictures when I get the chance,* she promised.

Good, I can't wait to hear all about it. Are you staying out of trouble? Holly questioned. She knew how Brigid attracted people in need, as if she was some sort of an invisible magnet. Hopefully she hadn't found a mystery to solve while she was supposed to be relaxing.

So far, she said. *Is your family nice?*

Holly wanted to type out a novel about the whole situation. How everyone was extremely nice, but she still felt like an outsider with her aunt. She was determined that by the time she headed home that was going to change.

Yes, everyone's really nice. It's just a little awkward sometimes, Holly admitted.

Give it time, Brigid responded. *They're probably not sure what to think of you, either.*

You're right, Holly replied. *Now go and enjoy the beach for me. Bring me back some seashells.* She finished her conversation with Brigid and set down her phone. She felt much better, even though Brigid really hadn't said much. Maybe it was just knowing she'd been thinking about Holly, even while she was on her honeymoon.

The sounds of movement in the hall told Holly that people were starting to stir. The sun was rising higher in the sky, and it wouldn't be long before she would have to put the family mystery on the back burner in order to focus on who framed Chloe.

She reached for the diary and began to read quickly. Skimming, she saw where Maggie mentioned Charlie a few more times. They'd meet somewhere away from her house, so he wouldn't find out where she lived. Holly couldn't believe how far her mother had gone to keep her secret. It all seemed so exhausting, and she was just reading it. She couldn't imagine how exhausting it would be telling lies and twisted truths to avoid telling anyone she was dating an older man and that he had no idea how young she was. She justified the whole thing because of how she felt about him, but Holly felt anxious for her just reading about it.

Frustrated with how her mother was handling the whole thing, Holly shoved the bookmark in the diary and slammed it shut. She'd read more later. It was time for her to get up. The smell of breakfast being cooked was luring her from her room.

CHAPTER SEVENTEEN

After breakfast, Steven and Lissa followed Holly back to her room. They were all still a little bleary eyed, but they were starting to come alive and prepare for the day ahead of them.

"I was thinking that we should try to talk to the rest of our suspects today. I'd really like to get this wrapped up as quickly as possible," Steven said after he shut the door.

"I agree," Holly said. "When it comes to real life cases, Brigid says that it's important to try and solve them as quickly as possible. You never know when someone may get rid of evidence that links them to a crime."

"Sure makes sense in this case," Lissa added. "Whoever did it not only has a blonde wig, but they also have Chloe's jacket. They'll probably want to get that back to her as soon as they can, so it really will look like she did it."

"Exactly what I was thinking," agreed Holly. "Tell Chloe to check and make absolutely sure the jacket isn't in her closet. I'm sure she's looked a million times already, but we want to make sure the real vandal hasn't already returned it."

"Good point," Steven said as he pulled out his phone to send her a message. "I'll check and see if Allison and Carrie are busy today.

Leah lives farther away, so we'll have to get a ride if we want to see her at her house." His fingers began to type furiously as he sent out his messages.

Holly nodded. "We'll get it figured out. Trust me. Everything will fall into place. Let's get dressed while you wait for their answers. It's probably better if we're ready, just in case someone has plans for the day."

Steven and Lissa headed for their own rooms to get dressed for the day, while Holly began to pull out her clothes. She tossed her favorite ripped jeans on the bed before digging to find the Smashing Pumpkins shirt she'd been waiting to wear. After getting dressed, she ran a brush through her hair and pulled it back into a messy bun.

It looked like it was going to be a nice day, but she could see from the trees swaying outside that it was a little breezy. Her hair blowing around in the wind would drive her nuts if she didn't pull it back. She slipped out of the bedroom and headed to the bathroom to brush her teeth. It wasn't long before the three of them met downstairs.

"I'm sorry, but your dad and I need the car today," Holly heard Katie telling Steven. "You guys can ride your bikes, can't you?"

"But what about Holly?" he asked as she entered the living room. "It's not like she's got a bike to ride."

"Holly can ride mine," Katie suggested. "It should be perfect for her. She and I are about the same height."

Steven looked a little disappointed, but Lissa smiled at him. "It's been a long time since we've ridden our bikes. It won't be that bad."

"That's the spirit," Katie said as she stood up from the couch. "I don't know how long we'll be gone, but there's plenty to eat for lunch." She gave each of them a hug goodbye and left.

"Have you heard back from anyone?" Holly asked as she sat down on the couch next to them.

"Allison says she's home. I thought we could go see her first," Steven said. "I'm still waiting to hear back from Leah and Carrie. Since it's summer vacation, who knows when they may get back to me. For all I know, they might both sleep until noon."

"There's no way Allison did it," Lissa said as they headed outside to the garage. There were white puffy clouds moving across the blue sky casting shadows in places. It was nice when one would move in front of the sun, giving them a moment of respite before shining brightly again.

"Why do you say that?" Holly asked as she watched her cousins uncover the bicycles. They were tucked in the far corner of the garage with a lot of other things in front of them like lawn chairs, a badminton set, and a couple of bags of potting soil.

"She's the smartest girl in her grade, well, besides Chloe," she shrugged.

"From the way Steph was talking, that would be a perfect reason," Steven pointed out. They'd finally gotten the bikes out and pushed one over to Holly. It was a deep red with a wire basket on the front. She couldn't imagine her aunt riding it, and from the amount of dust on it, she obviously hadn't for quite a while. They checked the tires before pushing the bikes out of the garage and closing the door behind them.

"What do you mean?" Lissa asked as they climbed on.

"Think about it. Stephanie said people were getting tired of always being the runner-up to Chloe. Maybe Allie wants to be noticed as being the smartest?" Steven shrugged. "Maybe she feels like Chloe is standing in her spotlight?"

"People have done worse for a lot less of a reason," Holly muttered. "If she wants to be seen as the smartest, that would be a big motive. Plus, I'd say whoever did this was pretty smart."

"Yeah, you have a point," Lissa said sadly.

After a short ride, they stopped in front of a small yellow house. Although the hedges were overgrown, the house and yard looked okay. It was more like the people who lived there just didn't have time to spend on lawn care. They dropped their bikes on the grass and headed over to the door. By the time they got to it, a girl was opening it.

"Hey, guys," she said as she pulled the door open. Steven introduced Holly, and they all followed her inside.

"Allison, we were wondering what you were doing yesterday morning?" Steven asked as she shut the door behind them with a soft click.

"Yesterday morning? My mom and I went to the mall together, why?" Allison answered with a confused look on her face.

"We don't believe Chloe was the one who vandalized the school. We're trying to help her figure out who did," Lissa explained.

"And you think I did?" Allison asked, raising her voice.

"Not at all," Holly said stepping in. "It's just that we want to be thorough and make sure we ask everyone." She gave Allison a reassuring smile that seemed to calm her down.

"Well, I was with my mom all day long yesterday. She had the day off so we spent some time together. I heard what happened, though. People are saying the school has proof it was her."

Steven shook his head. "They have a video, but you never see her face. We think someone was trying to make it look like it was her, so that she'd get in trouble. They may even be trying to get the bonfire cancelled."

They walked into the small living room and sat down on the couch. It was covered with a dark blue slipcover. and potted plants were everywhere in the room. The windows were wide open, letting in plenty of fresh air and sunshine.

"Too bad they didn't do it to get her grades to fall. That would help me a ton," Allison said dejectedly.

"Why's that?" Holly asked as she perched on the edge of the couch.

"I'm trying to be valedictorian this year. I want it so badly for my mom, but I think Chloe will probably end up beating me out for it," Allison said.

"Hey, you never know," Lissa said reassuringly. "As long as you don't give up you still have a chance."

Allison smiled weakly at her. "I wish I was as confident of that as you are."

"Lissa's right. Chloe isn't a robot. You never know, it might happen," Steven offered. "But if you give up, you definitely won't."

"I know," Allison sighed. "But I just want it so bad. You don't understand. My mom would have been valedictorian of her senior class if she hadn't gotten pregnant with me. All her dreams and hopes flew out the window because of me. I want to do it for her."

"That's beautiful," Holly said smiling. "But I bet your mom will be proud of you, no matter what. I mean, you and Chloe are probably pretty close in grades, right?"

"Yeah, I guess," Allison said.

"From what I hear, that's no small feat. Maybe you need to take it a little easier on yourself," Holly said.

Lissa nodded. "You're so much smarter than most of the kids in school. Don't let this get in your head and mess you up."

Allison began to bite her lip. "You think so?"

"They're right," Steven said. "How do you know you're not

getting in your own way? You may be shooting yourself in the foot worrying about her instead of doing your best."

She nodded. "Maybe you're right." She looked at each one of them and smiled. "Thanks, guys. Do you have any idea who it may be?"

"Not yet," Lissa said, shaking her head. "We still have a few more people to talk to."

"If you need any help, anything at all, let me know," Allison said. "Now that you've got me thinking about it, I would rather beat Chloe fair and square than let the vandalism thing get in her head and have her grades fall. Besides, the bonfire is fun, and I was kind of looking forward to watching the fireworks."

Just then, Steven's phone buzzed. "Good. It looks like Leah's on her way to Chloe's house," he said after checking the message. "That'll make it easier to talk to her, too."

"You think Leah may have done this? But she's best friends with Chloe," Allison said in a surprised tone of voice.

"Like we said, we're just making sure we cover all the bases," Holly explained.

"Still, I think my mind would be blown away if you found out it was her. I mean, they've been best friends for forever. If you can't trust your best friend, who can you trust?" Allison asked.

Steven's phone buzzed again and they turned and looked at him. "That was Carrie. She said she's over at the dog park with their Labrador retriever, and we can meet her there if we want to talk."

"How far is it?" asked Holly. Not that she minded riding a bike around town. It almost made her feel relaxed when she was pedaling, her hair blowing in the breeze. All those years of riding her bike around Cottonwood Springs made her feel very at home on a bike.

"It's not too far," explained Allison. "Just a few blocks east of here. It won't take much time by bike."

"Then let's go. Thanks for talking to us, Allison," Steven said as he stood up. The girls followed suit.

"Now you've got me curious. Let me know what you find out," Allison said as she walked them to the door.

"Don't worry, we will," Lissa said with a smile as they stepped back outside. When they heard the door close behind them, she said, "Looks like we can cross her off the list."

"I agree," Holly said. "Let's hope the final two on our list don't have alibis."

"For sure," Steven said. "Then who would we talk to?"

"I don't know," Holly said as they all got on their bikes. "We'll cross that bridge when we come to it."

"Is that something that happens often? All of the suspects having alibis?" Lissa asked.

"Not really, but once I was helping out with a mystery at school and one of the suspects lied about where she'd been at the time the crime took place.   It really threw me off until I spoke to someone else who told me the suspect hadn't been where she said she'd been," Holly recalled.

"That would be a big red flag," Steven said. "Was that the person who did it?"

"Sure was. Which leads to my next point. Eventually you'll find out if someone is lying. Usually you find out when they said they were somewhere. Then, if something's fishy, you ask the people they say can vouch for them. Most of the time, the other people will have no idea what you're talking about and rat them out." Holly knew it was more complicated than that, but for simplicity's sake she left it at that. Steven and Lissa probably weren't going to be doing any investigating after this, so it really didn't make any difference.

"With any luck, we won't have to go through all of that. I'm thinking we'll get this figured out today, thanks to your investigative skills, Holly," Lissa said brightly.

"I hope you're right, Lissa," Holly said as they continued to pedal.

CHAPTER EIGHTEEN

As they rode toward the dog park, Holly took in the sights. It was interesting to see just how different Springfield was from home and Denver. They were subtle, but there were definitely differences. Springfield didn't seem nearly as big, but it still had that big city vibe that Denver had with plenty to see and do. Holly hoped that once everything had calmed down, she'd be able to see what the city offered. Until then, she'd focus on helping Chloe.

As they rode up to the dog park, they slowed down a bit. She could tell Steven was scanning the area for Carrie. Once he spotted her, he pointed her out to Holly.

Carrie must have seen them coming, because she stood up from the bench where she'd been sitting and walked over to the fence so she could talk to them.

"Hi," she said with a bright smile, "what are you all out doing today?"

Steven introduced Holly to Carrie before jumping in about the vandalism. "Did you hear the bonfire's called off?"

"I sure did," she gasped. "I can't believe Chloe would do something like that," she said shaking her head. "I heard they even have a video that shows her doing it."

DIANNE HARMAN

"We don't think she did it," Steven said. "We think someone made it look like it was Chloe."

"Hmm," Carrie said as she tapped her manicured nail on her chin. Just then, a black Lab came running up to her, bumping her leg. She reached down and scratched behind his ear. "Who do you think might have done it?"

"We're not sure," Lissa interjected. "We're talking to everyone to see if anyone knows something that might help Chloe."

"I'm afraid I don't know anything," she shrugged.

"What did you do yesterday morning now that we're on vacation? Have you been staying busy?" Steven asked. He smiled at Holly and she nodded approvingly. He was starting to get the hang of asking questions in the right way, so that the person wouldn't be on the defensive.

"Yesterday? I was asleep all morning. I'd stayed up late the night before binge-watching a series. I don't think I got up until almost noon."

Holly made a mental note that Carrie didn't have an airtight alibi. Sure, she could have really been doing what she said, but she could also be trying to cover her tracks.

"Were you home all day alone?" he asked.

"No, my sister was there on and off," she said shaking her head. "What have you guys been up to?"

"Mainly getting to know our new cousin here," Lissa said as she touched Holly on her shoulder.

"New cousin? So you didn't know she was your cousin before now?" Carrie asked.

"It's kind of a long story," Holly explained. "The short version is that my mom moved away a long time ago and never talked about her family. After she died, I found out about these guys." She smiled at them both. "It's kind of nice, actually."

"I'm sorry about your mom," Carrie said. "Are you going to move here?"

"Nope, just visiting," she said. "What's your dog's name?"

"This is Willie," Carrie said as she patted him on his side. "He's the family dog, but I like to bring him here sometimes. He loves playing with all the other dogs. I swear, he's probably got more friends than I do," she chuckled.

Holly needed to figure out if Carrie had some sort of motive for wanting to ruin Chloe's reputation. Since she didn't have anyone to vouch for where she specifically was at the time of the vandalism, she was still a suspect.

"It's kind of crazy that someone would do this to Chloe," Holly began. "Do you have any idea who would do this?"

Carrie scoffed. "To be honest, I'm not so sure she didn't do it," she admitted.

Steven looked surprised. "Why would you even say that?"

Carrie rolled her eyes. "Personally, I don't think she's the goody-goody everyone else does. I bet she thought she could do anything and decided to do it just for fun. She probably didn't count on the cameras being there."

"Does that mean you're not a fan of Chloe's?" Holly asked.

"Honestly? Not really. I mean, I don't have a direct reason to not like her. It's just...," she paused as if she were choosing her words carefully. "I don't get why everyone makes such a big deal over her. Yeah, she throws a party every year. Big whoop. Anybody can do that, but what I really don't understand is why the guys are always making such a big deal over her," she grumbled.

Holly bet there was a lot more to it than what Carrie was saying. From the sounds of it, she resented everyone paying attention to Chloe.

"Well, she does always try to help out," Lissa said. "And she's good at a lot of stuff."

"Yeah, which makes it harder for anyone else who would like to be noticed," Carrie spat. She seemed to collect herself, and she cleared her throat. "I just don't think she's all that big of a deal," she said simply.

Holly had a feeling there was some serious animosity on Carrie's part. She mentally moved Carrie up to the top of the suspect list.

"Well, I think we're going to take a break and get something to drink. Have fun with Willie," Steven said quickly before climbing back on his bike.

"Thanks," Carrie said brightly as she gave them a small wave.

Steven led them to a nearby gas station where they parked their bikes and headed inside.

"That was a little weird," Lissa said breaking the silence.

"Yeah, there doesn't seem to be any love lost there," Holly agreed. "I think we may need to look into her some more."

"I agree," Steven said as they headed for the soft drink cooler. "Want something to drink? My treat."

Each of them grabbed a can of soda before they stepped over to the checkout counter and Steven paid. Once outside, he took a long drink as he stared at the dog park.

"What are you thinking about?" Holly asked before taking a drink of her soda.

"I'm thinking Carrie's problem is all because of Kyle," Steven said, still thinking.

"Oh?" Lissa asked. "Why? I thought Carrie and Kyle were just friends."

"They are," Steven agreed. "But I'm starting to think that maybe Carrie wants more. Kyle's made it no secret he wants to date Chloe. Maybe Carrie tried to ask him out and he shot her down?"

Holly shrugged. "It's always possible. Jealousy is a pretty big motivation for trying to frame someone."

"Exactly," Steven said. He slid his soda can into the holder on his bike. "Why don't we head over to Chloe's so we can catch Leah. I doubt it's her because they're best friends, and Carrie just made it so obvious she doesn't like her."

"Yeah, but we should probably make sure," Lissa said nodding.

"I agree. It's better to be safe than just assume," Holly pointed out.

"Okay. Let's go," Steven said as he turned his bike around.

CHAPTER NINETEEN

When the three of them rode their bikes up to Chloe's house, they saw Chloe and Leah sitting on the porch, enjoying the fresh air. Chloe introduced Holly and Leah before they started to chat.

"Leah was just telling me about some of her paintings," Chloe beamed. "She's been taking an online class to learn how to paint watercolors, and she brought some with her to show me."

"Really?" Lissa asked. "That's cool. I've always wanted to learn, but I've never taken the time. I'd love to see them."

"Yeah, go get them, Leah. I really want to see them, too," Chloe said.

"They're in my backpack in the house. Hang on, and I'll go get them," she said as she stood up and went in the front door.

"How's the investigation going?" Chloe asked quietly.

"We found something out, but I don't want to say anything in front of Leah," Steven whispered. Chloe nodded right before Leah reappeared. In her hands were paintings of different types of flowers and leaves. She passed them around and everyone took the time to marvel at each one.

"These are amazing, Leah," Chloe said smiling. "Who knew you had such a talent?"

Leah shrugged. "I don't know. You really like them?" she asked with a faint blush on her cheeks.

"Leah, these are amazing," Holly said nodding. "You really should continue with this. It's obvious you're very talented. Who knows where it will lead?"

"Thanks," she said, clearly proud of herself. "I didn't think they were all that good."

"Are you kidding?" Chloe said, gaping. "My best friend is an artist! Who else can say that?" she asked. "You've got to paint one for me."

"Okay," Leah said, smiling. "I'll be back in a couple of minutes. I want to put these away and while I'm inside, I'm going to the bathroom."

Chloe nodded as her friend disappeared back inside her house. Once they were sure she wasn't coming right back out, Steven turned to Chloe.

"We're starting to wonder if it wasn't Carrie," he said softly. "It looks like she's not a big fan of yours, and she doesn't have anyone who can verify where she was yesterday morning."

Chloe nodded. "I can see her doing it. She's always seemed a bit standoffish with me."

"We still should find out what Leah was doing, though," Holly pointed out. "You never want to assume anything." She turned to Chloe, "Everyone else has someone who can say they weren't at the school during the time of the vandalism."

Chloe nodded. "I also checked my room top to bottom this morning, just like you asked. My jacket is still gone. Leah's the first person who's been over since it happened."

"Good, make sure you keep checking after each time you have a visitor. I don't think we should let anyone else know we're looking into this. I'd like them to think they got away with it," Steven said. "After the way Carrie reacted, I started running it over in my mind. If whoever did it knows we're looking into it, they'll be very careful with what they say, but if they think they pulled it off…"

"Then they might not be as sneaky. Good thinking," Chloe said.

"Could you show me that video, again?" Holly asked. "Now that I've met everyone, I want to see if I notice something different."

"Sure," Chloe nodded. "Let's just wait until Leah gets back, and then I'll make an excuse. I don't have it on my phone anymore, but it's still on my laptop."

"We'll keep her occupied while you two are busy," Lissa offered. "Won't do any good if she goes looking for you and finds out what you're doing."

"I think she's coming," Chloe said as she leaned back toward the window she was seated in front of. Within a matter of moments, Leah was back. Lissa was asking Leah about the watercolor class she was taking when Chloe interrupted. "Hey, Holly. Didn't I promise to show you the pictures from the museum? I remember you saying you weren't sure if you wanted to go."

"That's right," Holly said, playing along. "I'd really appreciate that."

"Come with me, and I'll show you. It'll only take a minute. We'll be right back, guys," she said as she motioned Holly towards the front door. When they were inside, Holly followed Chloe to her room.

She pushed the door open and Holly was surprised by the soft light blue color on the walls. It wasn't something she'd have ever imagined on bedroom walls, but it was very pretty.

"I really like the color in here," Holly said.

"Thanks. My parents thought I was crazy when they saw the swatch, but they let me do it anyway. Mom admitted after it was all done that it was pretty," she chuckled. She walked over to a white desk that held her laptop while Holly continued to look around.

All of the trim was white along with the floating shelves that held rows of picture frames. Chloe's closet was stuffed with clothing, each piece crammed in. It was inconsistent with the rest of her room, which was spotless.

"Here you go," Chloe said after she pulled up the video. Holly moved closer and began to watch as Chloe stepped back. She wasn't sure exactly what she was looking for. There had to be something, something that proved the person in the video wasn't Chloe.

Then, she found it. When she had a clear shot, she paused the video. Shoes. She tried to get a closer look at the shoes the person was wearing in the video. They looked like athletic shoes. Turning, she looked at Chloe's feet. She was wearing flats.

"Chloe?" Holly began, but she was interrupted by Chloe's gasp.

"Oh my gosh," Chloe said as she rushed over to her closet. She pushed everything aside and pulled something out. When she turned around, Holly saw it was the jacket from the video.

"The jacket," Holly said, wide-eyed.

"Yeah, and it wasn't there this morning," Chloe said lifting it up.

"Are you sure?" Holly asked. She moved across the room and touched one of the embroidered stars. It was much prettier in person than in the video.

"I'm absolutely positive. I went through everything in my closet this morning to be sure." She gasped. "That means it was Leah."

"I'd have to agree. It sure looks that way. Tell me, do you always wear flats?" Holly asked.

"Most of the time, unless I'm doing something like cross country where I need a specific kind of shoe. Why?"

"Because the person in this video is wearing athletic shoes. I'm willing to bet if we look at shoes, it will give us a clue who the vandal is." Holly moved back over to the laptop and took a screenshot before sending it to herself. "Now I'll have a picture of the shoes. The film is in black and white, but it will still give us a better idea of who it may be. Do you know if Leah or Carrie has shoes like those?"

"Honestly, I'm not sure," Chloe admitted. "But we can find out if Leah does if we can come up with an excuse to go to her house."

Holly nodded. "And if we could sneak into her room, maybe we can find out if she has a certain blonde wig," she pointed out.

"But how can we convince her that we want to go to her house?" Chloe asked, more to herself than anything. "Oh, I've got it! She has this game that takes a lot of people to play. I'll suggest we go over to her house and play it."

"Doesn't she live farther away?" Holly asked. She wasn't sure if she wanted to ride a bike all over Springfield.

"Yeah, but don't worry. I can drive us over there. Come on, let's do this." Chloe shoved the jacket back in the closet and hurried downstairs. "Just let me handle this part."

When they joined the others outside, everyone was laughing at something Steven had said.

"Hey, guys, I have a great idea!" Chloe exclaimed as she skipped to her seat. "Leah's got this really neat game, but it's only fun when there's a group of people. Why don't we go over to your house, Leah, and play? I'll drive." She turned to Leah, "We can sit in your backyard at that big table you have outside."

Leah shrugged. "If you guys want to, that's fine with me."

Steven and Lissa looked from Chloe to Holly. Holly gave them a slight nod letting them know to play along.

"Sounds good. Can we stash our bikes here?" Steven asked.

"Of course," Chloe said. "Let me grab my keys and lock the house, then we can go."

"I'll go ahead and meet you there," Leah said as she walked out to her little car. "I'll see you guys there." She gave them a small wave as she climbed behind the wheel before backing down the driveway and pulling away.

Holly turned to Steven and Lissa. "The jacket is back."

"Are you serious?" Steven asked. "But Carrie?"

"I know," Holly said nodding. "I'm right there with you. But for now, let's see how this goes. We'll explain it all on the way over."

Lissa and Steven nodded as they began to move their bikes. Holly had a feeling they were about to put all the pieces in place. One way or another, they were going to figure this out.

CHAPTER TWENTY

"I still can't believe it," Chloe said, shaking her head. Holly couldn't help but feel sorry for her. Granted, they still didn't have any real proof yet that Leah had done it, but the appearance of her jacket after Leah had been alone inside, seemed to make a believer out of Chloe. "She's been my best friend for forever. Why would she want to get me in trouble?"

"Let's not jump ahead of ourselves," Holly said from the back seat of the little black sedan. "The appearance of your jacket isn't exactly a smoking gun."

"I know, but still," Chloe said as she navigated through traffic.

"Try to relax," Steven said as he placed his hand on Chloe's shoulder. He was sitting in the front with her, a concerned look on his face. "The important thing is, if she did it, she's not going to get away with it."

"That's right," said Lissa. "We'll find the proof we need to clear you of all of this."

"Thanks, guys. I guess I'm still just so surprised that she would do something like this." Chloe didn't take her eyes from the road, but Holly could see in the rearview mirror that they were getting watery. She felt so sorry for her. Holly wasn't sure what else she could do but help her find out the truth.

"We all know the plan, right?" Steven asked as he turned in his seat so he could see everyone.

Holly nodded. "Yep, this is going to go like clockwork. With any luck, we'll have Chloe's name cleared before dinner."

"That would be amazing," Chloe sighed. "My parents told me if I can prove that I had nothing to do with this, the bonfire will be back on. I'm just grateful they're giving me the chance to clear my name."

"Well, it helps that you've been such a good person, I'm sure," Steven said with a small smile.

Chloe looked over at him and returned it with one of her own. "Thanks. I really appreciate what you've done for me. I know you probably have a lot of other things you'd rather be doing right now than helping me." She put on her turn signal and they pulled onto a residential street. Every house in the neighborhood looked pretty much the same.

"Nah," Steven said. "It's no trouble."

"If this works out, I'm going to owe you all big time," she said emphatically. "Here we are." She came to a stop in front of one of the many brown two-story homes. This one had a swing in the front yard, but aside from that it looked just like the rest of them.

As they were getting out the car, Leah opened the front door of the house. "My mom should be getting off work soon, so she'll be here later on." She pulled out her phone and looked at the time. "Actually, she may be on her way home now."

"That's okay, she won't bother us," Chloe said brightly. Holly was amazed at how quickly she was able to go from being hurt to being perky, but then again, she probably knew if she didn't act the way she normally did it might tip Leah off. It was best if she didn't suspect a thing.

"I already have the game out on the table in the back yard," she said hitching her thumb over her shoulder. "Come on in."

They followed her through the front door, and she shut it behind them. The house had an open floor plan which allowed someone to see all the way through to the back yard from the front door. The group followed Leah outside and began to sit down while she explained the game. Holly knew this was the perfect opportunity.

"I'm really sorry, but may I use your bathroom?" she asked.

"Sure," Leah said stopping to answer Holly while she was pulling the game pieces from the box. "I can show you."

"No, you go ahead and keep setting the game up. I'll show her," Chloe insisted.

"Are you sure?" she asked.

"Of course," Chloe said with a bright smile. "You explain it to them while I take her in and show her where it is. Come on, Holly." They stood up and headed back into the house.

"Perfect timing," Chloe said to Holly as she shut the door. "It gave us a great reason to leave her there, and she'll be so busy she won't notice how long we're gone."

"That's what I was thinking," Holly said. "But we better make it quick."

Chloe nodded and they hurried through the house and up the stairs. Once there, Holly pushed open a door with paper flowers and stars all over it. Inside, the room was fairly neat for a teenage girl. There were clothes hanging from the chair in front of a desk, but otherwise it was quite clean. The walls were coral pink and the bedspread was a bright white. On the far wall there was a collage with pictures and things cut from magazines covering most of it.

"Okay, so we need to look for those shoes and a wig, right?"

Chloe asked.

"Yep. If we could find both of them, that would be terrific," Holly said nodding.

Chloe began to search while Holly thought about where she would hide a wig if this was her room. Her eyes slid over drawers, a night stand, and dresser, but she quickly dismissed them. Too obvious of a place to hide something. She pulled the curtains out and looked behind them while Chloe began to search the closet.

"I never realized how many pairs of shoes she had," Chloe said as she began to pull shoeboxes from the bottom of the closet.

Holly looked over and saw the stack of boxes. "Wow, I don't even keep mine in boxes. I'm impressed," she admitted.

Chloe shrugged. "We've both done it for a while now. Helps keep them a little nicer."

Holly turned back to the room and lifted the blankets on the side of the bed. Running her hand along under the mattress, her fingers searched but found nothing. She got down on her hands and knees and began looking under the bed.

"I think I may have found the shoes," Chloe said quickly. She lifted a pair from the box and held them up for Holly to see.

Holly pulled out her phone and compared the two. Both had a light stripe that ran along the length and brightly colored shoe laces. Although the image on her phone was black and white, it looked like the same shoe. "I think it's the same," she nodded.

"Then we've got her," Chloe said.

"Not yet," Holly said as she bent back over to continue searching under the bed. "She could always use the excuse someone else had the same shoes."

"You're right, I didn't think of that," Chloe said, dejectedly.

"If we find both the shoes and the wig, that would be all the proof we'd need to confront her," Holly said. "There's a lot of stuff under here," she mumbled.

"Here, let me help," Chloe said as she knelt down at the other end of the bed. Her eyes looked around before stopping near where Holly was. "What's that?" she asked pointing.

"What?" Holly asked as she tried to crane her neck to see what Chloe was pointing at.

"There, on the left. It looks like it's tucked between the frame and the box springs," she said squinting.

Holly began to run her hand along the underside of the bed until she felt something plastic. Gingerly, she touched the item, trying to determine what it was just from touch.

"I don't know," she admitted. "Here, let me try to pull it out." With a slight tug it came free, and she pulled it out. When she turned it over in her hands, she saw that it was a flat black bag with a zip seal. She looked at Chloe curiously, but Chloe just shrugged.

"Open it," Chloe said.

Holly pulled the bag open and peeked inside. "This might be the wig," she said carefully as she reached inside. She saw something that looked white with netting across it. As she pulled it out from the bag, she noticed it looked like hair with a hair net around it.

Chloe gasped. "That's it, isn't it?"

Holly found the edge of the netting and pulled it back. The white blonde hair tumbled down in a cascade. Both girls' eyes became wide as they looked at each other.

"Well," Holly said. "I think we know who the vandal is."

"Yeah, I guess so," said Chloe. "Now I want to know why."

CHAPTER TWENTY-ONE

"What is this, Leah?" Chloe asked as she flung open the door to the backyard. In her fist was the platinum blonde wig that bore a striking resemblance to Chloe's hair. Under the other arm was a shoebox.

Steven and Lissa looked as shocked as Leah when her eyes landed on the wig. Holly could almost see the realization that she'd been caught flicker across Leah's face, then the surprised look changed into one of resolve. She didn't say a word, instead, she stayed where was, leaning over the table.

"Is that a wig?" Lissa asked.

"What were you doing in my room?" Leah croaked out as she straightened up.

"And what about these?" Chloe asked as she flipped open the shoe box. "These are the shoes someone wore to dress up like me and vandalize the school." She dropped the box to the ground. "And not to mention the fact that my hoodie has been missing for forever, and amazingly somehow finds its way back into my closet after you went into my house alone! That's a little too much coincidence for me." By the time she got to the end, Chloe was yelling.

"So what?" Leah spat at her. "It's about time you fell off that high horse of yours."

"Are you serious?" Chloe scoffed. She took one step toward Leah. Steven and Lissa quickly rose to their feet and went over to where Chloe was standing. She was beginning to clench her hands into fists. "What have I ever done to you, Leah? Besides listen to you cry about boys and whine about how fat you're getting."

"Okay, Chloe," Holly said as she stepped towards her. "That's enough. Calm down."

"What's going on out here?" an older woman asked as she opened the back door. She was still wearing her scrubs from work. "I just pulled up and heard loud voices. Want to tell me what this is all about?"

"Mom, it's nothing," Leah began, but Chloe cut her off.

"Leah's the one who vandalized the school, not me," she said, interrupting Leah.

Her mother looked from one girl to the other and then noticed Steven, Lissa, and Holly. "Okay, someone needs to explain to me what's going on. Right now." She crossed her arms.

"I will," Holly said as Leah and Chloe started to argue again.

"And, forgive me, but who are you?" Leah's mother asked.

"I'm Steven and Lissa's cousin, ma'am." Holly cleared her throat and began to speak. "As you probably know, someone looking like Chloe vandalized the school. Chloe swore she didn't do it, so Steven, Lissa, and I have been helping her try to find out who it really was, so she can clear her name. Her parents called off the bonfire because of the vandalism, and she was devastated."

Leah's mother nodded. "Yes, I've heard some of this."

"Okay, so we started looking for the jacket that was worn in the video, because it's been missing from Chloe's closet for a little while. Today, after Leah came to visit Chloe, the jacket magically appeared back in her closet. She'd looked this morning and it wasn't there. Chloe thought up a plan so we could see if there was any evidence in Leah's room.

"Chloe asked Leah if we could come over here. Earlier, I looked at the vandal's shoes on the video and took a picture of them. You see, Chloe almost always wears flats and the person in the video is wearing athletic shoes." Holly held up the image on her phone, so Leah's mother could see what she was talking about.

Her eyes became wide as she recognized the shoes. She looked at Leah before she said, "Go on."

"The last thing was the hair. We assumed that whoever did it must have worn a wig." She gestured toward the wig still tightly clenched in Chloe's fist. "We found that wig hidden under Chloe's bed."

Leah's mother took the wig from Chloe and looked at it carefully before bending over and picking up the shoes. She put the wig in the box before closing it and tucking it under her arm. "Leah, what do you have to say for yourself?"

Leah opened her mouth, but no sound came out. She looked as though she were planning to argue, but then she evidently decided it wouldn't do her any good. "It's true," she finally said.

"I see," her mother said as she stepped forward. Her voice became low as she sternly spoke. "You will fix this. Today. Call the school and tell them everything, as well as apologizing for vandalizing the lockers. Then, you are to call Chloe' parents and explain everything to them, as well as apologize to them. Chloe is supposed to be your best friend, Leah. How could you do this to her?"

Leah began to speak, but her mother silenced her. "I don't want to hear it right now." She turned to Chloe, Holly, Lissa, and Steven. "I'm so sorry she did this, Chloe. Please accept my apology, but I'm going to have to ask you to leave while I further discuss this with my daughter."

"Yes, Mrs. Cortez," Chloe said politely. They quietly slipped through the house and headed for the car.

"Are you okay, Chloe?" Steven asked.

"I-I," she began but her voice broke and she began to cry. "No."

He pulled her into his arms, and she went willingly, her tears turning into sobs. He spoke softly into her hair, speaking consoling words to help her relax. Her shoulders shook as she continued to cry. Soon she pulled away and the other two girls patted her on the back.

"Why don't you let Steven drive?" Lissa asked. "He's really not that bad, and I think you need a little time to pull yourself together."

She glanced from Lissa to Steven, her eyes red and puffy. "Okay."

They climbed into the car, Steven behind the wheel, and Chloe in the passenger seat. She opened the glove box and pulled out a small package of tissues.

"Well, at least now your name is cleared," Lissa said, "and that's a good thing." Holly couldn't help but feel terrible for Chloe. To be best friends with someone and then have them do something like that had to really hurt. And why did Leah throw everything away just to get even with Chloe and for what? Because Chloe was better at something than she was? Maybe a boy? Was what she'd done really worth the loss of her reputation and Chloe's friendship?

Holly knew people threw away relationships all the time over the slightest things. A misunderstanding or rumor. It often didn't take much.

"Yeah, I guess so," Chloe sniffled. "I just can't believe she did it. Out of everyone who came to my house that day, she was the last one I ever thought would do something like this."

"It will all work out in the end," Steven said softly. Chloe turned and looked at him, a look of genuine appreciation on her face.

"I don't know what I would have done without you, Steven," she said. "Oh, and you two, of course," she said looking over her shoulder at Lissa and Holly.

When she turned back around, Lissa gave Holly a pointed look and wagged her eyebrows at her. Holly couldn't help but giggle. It did seem as though Chloe was starting to see Steven in a different light.

"This whole thing has me feeling totally confused," Chloe said as she turned toward the passenger window. "It's like my world has come crumbling down, and I don't know what's happening."

"Give it time," Holly said. "Sometimes you just need to keep your head above water while you wait for everything to settle down. Friends fight, people lie, nobody's perfect. If anything, it's when a person tries to be perfect that things really go downhill. Before long everything just piles up and then explodes."

Chloe was quiet for a moment, letting it all sink in. "Maybe you're right. Maybe it's my fault."

"That's not what I was saying at all," Holly objected.

"I know," Chloe began. "But I heard what Leah said. She thought that I thought I was better than everyone else. That wasn't it at all, but maybe if I had done things differently..."

"Hey, don't even go there," Steven said quickly. "You did nothing wrong. You were always nice to everyone and always tried to help people. You can't worry about how other people took it. I've never seen you do or say anything unkind to anyone. If anything, sometimes you were too nice."

"How could I have been too nice?" Chloe asked as she turned towards him.

"You don't have to help people that don't try. Sometimes, people need to learn from their mistakes. You don't need to invite absolutely everyone to your bonfire if you don't want to." He sighed heavily as he turned a corner. "If anything, maybe you need to be a little more selfish. Life's too short, you know?"

Chloe began to nod slowly. "Maybe you're right. But right now, all I want is a big greasy cheeseburger and some chili cheese fries."

Everyone laughed before Steven said, "That sounds great, but let's find your parents and tell them the good news first."

CHAPTER TWENTY-TWO

"Thank you so much for all of your help," Chloe said as she walked Holly, Lissa, and Steven outside. They'd just finished explaining everything to Chloe's parents after they'd gotten a call from Leah. "Now I can text everyone and tell them the bonfire is back on," she said with a smile.

"Are you sure you're going to be okay?" Steven asked.

Chloe nodded. "I will be, thanks to you."

The front door opened and Chloe's brother, Seth, jogged out to them. "I just heard the news," he said with a grin. "Congratulations, you guys saved the bonfire."

"We could have never done it without Holly," Lissa said. "If it wasn't for her, we wouldn't have known where to even begin."

"Is that so?" Seth asked as he walked up in front of Holly. "Then I guess I owe you one, Holly."

Holly waved her hand, dismissing him. "It really wasn't that big of a deal," she said easily.

"Why don't I take you out sometime? I can show you a good time," he said as he raised one eyebrow.

"Thanks, but I don't think so," Holly said as she stepped back. "I have a boyfriend back home, and I don't think he'd like me going out with another guy while I'm gone." Holly wasn't exactly used to guys hitting on her so blatantly, and the whole thing was making her feel more than a little uncomfortable.

"Oh, come on," he said as he grabbed her hand. "You don't have to tell him. Nobody has to know, it can be our little secret."

"But I'd know," Holly insisted as she pulled her hand away. "And I'm not like that."

Seth raised his hands in surrender. "Your choice, but if you change your mind, you know where I am." He nodded to Steven and Lissa before turning and heading back in the house.

"I don't think he knew what to think about a girl turning him down," Chloe chuckled. "That's not something that happens very often to him."

Holly shrugged. "Sorry, I'm just not into the pushy type."

"Me neither," Chloe said as her eyes drifted over to where Steven was standing.

Holly noticed that the two of them were standing fairly close together. "Hey Lissa, why don't you and I give Chloe and Steven a little time together," she said.

Lissa looked at Chloe and Steven and her eyes grew wide. "Yeah, I think you're right." She raised her voice a little and said, "Holly and I are going to be over here when you're ready, Steven."

"Oh, uh, okay," Steven said. He didn't even look towards his sister and Holly as they slowly neared the corner with their bikes.

"Chloe seems like she likes Steven," Holly said once they were out of earshot.

"It's kind of looking that way, isn't it?" Lissa said easily. "I guess that's a good thing, though. He's had a crush on her for forever. Maybe this whole thing is making her see him in a different light. You think?" she asked.

"Maybe. Or maybe it's the fact that she sees holding herself to these high standards isn't doing her any favors. Maybe she's decided that it's time to enjoy herself a little." Holly wasn't sure and really, it didn't matter. What did matter was that Chloe's name had been cleared. If she was able to see a good thing that had been right in front of her face the whole time, even better.

"What do you think they're talking about?" Lissa asked as they stopped at the corner. They both turned and glanced over at Steven and Chloe before turning away again.

"I don't know, but it looks pretty serious," Holly said. Both Steven and Chloe were gazing intently at each other. They were mere inches apart and it looked as though they had forgotten that anyone else was around. Holly thought it was actually kind of sweet.

"Oh my gosh," Lissa gasped as Chloe reached up toward Steven's face and lifted her chin. Steven lowered his face to hers and they gently kissed. From where Holly stood, it didn't look like an earth-shattering kiss, just a simple touch of the lips. But from the look on Chloe and Steven's faces, their world had just shifted. Chloe's cheeks flared crimson before she dashed inside her house leaving Steven standing there on her lawn in disbelief.

He began pushing his bike toward his sister and cousin, completely oblivious to them. He didn't say a word as he passed by them.

"What was that all about?" Lissa asked as they caught up to him. None of them seemed in a hurry to ride their bikes. It was as if they needed a little more time to process everything that had happened that day.

"Huh?" Steven asked as though he were snapping out of it. "Oh, well, Chloe asked me out on a date," he admitted with a far-away look in his eye.

"You have a date with Chloe?" Lissa asked in astonishment.

"Yeah, I guess I do," he said with a smile. He seemed to be coming around. "She also said she's going to talk to her grandparents about maybe moving up the bonfire, so Holly can go, too. She said it's only right since she helped make sure it was back on."

"She doesn't have to do that," Holly said, embarrassed. "I was just trying to help."

"And she's extremely grateful," Steven said.

"Yeah, we could see that," Lissa scoffed. "I'm just surprised. She must really be grateful if she's willing to kiss a troll like you," she teased.

"Hey now, people say we look just alike," Steven said over his shoulder. "If I'm a troll, what does that make you?"

"We do not look alike," Lissa insisted. "Remember, we don't have the same biological mother. Now come on, let's hurry up and get home. I'm starving."

The three of them climbed on their bikes and began to pedal for home.

CHAPTER TWENTY-THREE

"Dinner's almost ready," Katie called from the kitchen as they entered the house.

Steven headed directly for the kitchen, but Holly placed her hand on Lissa's arm. "I'm going upstairs to read in my mom's diary until it's dinner time," she said.

Lissa nodded. "I understand. Would you like me to come with you?"

Holly shook her head. "No, that's okay. I just want to read some more. I think I'm getting close to figuring out what really happened. She's been mentioning a guy. Maybe it's leading up to something with him."

"I hope so. I'm curious about what happened, too. I mean, it seems like something pretty bad had to happen for your mom to not ever want to come back here, and my mom not want to talk about it," Lissa said with an anxious look on her face. "Good luck."

"Thanks," Holly said with a small smile. "Let me know when it's time to eat." Lissa nodded, and Holly hurried upstairs. The diary had been on her mind most of the day, at least when they weren't involved in catching Leah. That had been something else.

Closing the door to her room, Holly flopped down on the bed and pulled out the diary. She read for a while and then things started to get interesting.

In the diary, Maggie and the guy she referred to as C continue to get serious. She's seventeen at this point and falling in love with him. He seems to say all the right things, makes her feel special, all of it. She goes on and on about how she wants to tell him just how she feels, but she's nervous to be the one to say it first. All the girls at school tell her that you have to let the guy say it first, but she's not sure.

Multiple times she wrote how she'd almost said it that night. The words would be on her lips, but instead, she would hold them in. Her insecurity was obvious on every page that Holly read, and then she read something that really surprised her.

It happened. C and I made love. It was my first time. I didn't tell him that, but I think he figured it out. He was pretty quiet afterwards. Especially after I told him I loved him. I couldn't wait anymore. While we were lying there together it just came out. Shortly after that I had to leave.

He still doesn't know how old I am. I probably should have said something before now, but I don't think it would have mattered. Even though he hasn't said it, I'm sure he loves me. He's probably just being careful. Maybe someone hurt him badly in the past. Either way, I let him know how I felt and that was all that mattered.

Holly felt her heart sinking for her mother. It was obvious to Holly that it hadn't ended well, knowing what had happened to her mother. She found herself wanting to reach into the diary and shake her mother, look her in the eyes and tell her to stop putting her happiness in someone else's hands. The whole thing seemed like a predictable daytime soap opera. With a heavy heart, Holly continued to read.

There was more of the same until finally, Maggie begins to mention not feeling well. She'd tried to get together with C, but he started having to work late, or he was tired and couldn't see her.

Horrified, Holly understood what was happening.

I went home early again today. Threw up halfway into first hour. The girl who sits next to me was joking when she asked if I was pregnant, but the possibility cut through me. I hadn't even thought about it. I thought I had a stomach bug. I stopped by the pharmacy on the way home and grabbed a pregnancy kit. Good thing I hadn't been eating lunch, so I could afford the kit.

As soon as I got home, I took the test. There was no way I could wait. I sat in the bathroom, watching as the two lines that meant I was pregnant instantly appeared.

I have to admit I felt like I was going to pass out. I never thought something like this would happen to me. I didn't think I'd really have to worry about it my first time. Now, I have to find a way to tell C. Maybe he'll know what to do. But this means I'm going to have to tell him how old I am. He'll find out sooner or later. It's probably better if I tell him now rather than wait until I'm painted into a corner. It's a little soon, but I'm sure he'll do the right thing. He's such a good guy and I love him so much.

Holly couldn't help but shake her head. She was having a hard time connecting the woman in the diary with her mother. They seemed like two completely different people. This one seemed so young and innocent, so very trusting. How could a woman go from being this person to someone who would abandon her young child at home to go out and get a fix? It made Holly painfully aware of how vulnerable people really are.

All the time she'd spent in the public library when she was younger had allowed her to read quite a few books she normally wouldn't have been interested in. Because of that, and her mother, she'd read a few on addiction and the triggers that can cause an addict to spiral downward.

Was whatever had made her mother go to Colorado and isolate herself also what made her turn to drugs and alcohol? Had she been trying to block the world out, numbing herself to the pain? If she did, then it actually explained quite a bit. The only way to try and find out was to keep reading.

Well, things didn't go as planned. I wanted to visit C tonight and tell him everything. Instead, he told me how we were going to have to break up because he was moving to Denver for work. I told him I wanted to see him, but he said he just didn't have the time and that it was probably better this way. At first my heart shattered into a million pieces, but then I remembered what I needed to tell him. I tried to get a word in, but he hung up before I got a chance. But that's okay. I'll just find a way to get to his house in the next day or so. Then I can tell him in person.

She sounded so optimistic Holly couldn't help but hold out hope. Maybe things did work out and then something else happened. It was always possible. She scanned through the diary for the next mention of the situation.

I showed up at his place, but it was empty. Thankfully, his neighbor had his forwarding address, so at least I know where he moved to. I thought about just sending a letter to explain everything to him, but then I had a brilliant idea. Of course, I'm not going to be able to take this diary with me. I'm not taking much. Just whatever I can fit in my backpack and all the money I've been saving. I decided I'm going to go to Denver.

I told Katie and she was angry. I told her the whole thing. That I was in love, pregnant and going to be with him. She told me I was crazy. That I should stay here. That maybe it was still soon enough that I could get an abortion. I told her there was no way I could do that. I know the baby isn't very big yet and that some may argue it's not even alive yet, but I don't care.

For me, that baby is already a piece of me. I couldn't get rid of the baby any more than I could get rid of an ear or a toe. Plus, I don't want to. She'll see. I'll go to Denver, show up on C's doorstep and he'll be so happy to see me, he won't question how I got there. He might be disappointed when he finds out I'm not eighteen yet, but I think he'll come around. Anyway, it won't be long before I'm eighteen.

Katie threatened to tell our parents, but I made her promise not to until I was gone. She had to at least give me a head start. I asked her to not tell them I'm pregnant, but I could tell by the look on her face she was probably going to, anyway. Oh well. When I'm out of here, they won't be able to find me to stop me. Wish me luck, diary. I think I may need it.

That was it. Nothing else after that. Just empty page after empty page.

"That's it?" Holly said aloud.

She flipped through all of the remaining pages, hoping to find something to fill in the rest of the story, but there was nothing. That's when she realized where she was and who was downstairs. All she had to do was go ask her Aunt Katie if she actually told her parents. She wanted to know what they'd done and if her mother ever found the guy and told him.

Holly was nervous about asking Katie, but she knew she had enough knowledge now to press for the right answers. She felt as if the answer to all of her questions was downstairs.

CHAPTER TWENTY-FOUR

"I was just about to come get you for dinner," Lissa said from the bottom of the stairs as she saw Holly coming down. "How did the diary reading go?"

"I swear I have more questions than answers, but I read the entire thing," Holly said as she made her way down the stairs.

"What are you going to do now?" Lissa asked.

"The only thing I can think to do," she said as she got to the bottom of the stairs. "Ask your mom."

The two girls entered the dining room just as everyone was beginning to sit down.

"I heard you guys helped Chloe clear her name," Katie said as she set the lasagna down in the center of the table. "Great job. I'm very proud of all of you."

"Sounds like we need to celebrate," Allen said as he began to dish out the food. "Maybe we'll go sightseeing tomorrow and hit a restaurant while we're out."

"That sounds great," Holly began. "But you might change your mind here in a little bit."

Confused, Katie and Allen turned to her. "Why would we do that?" Katie asked.

"Well, I've been reading my mother's old diary, and I have a lot of questions," she admitted. "I know you don't like answering my questions, and I don't mean to upset you. It's just...," she searched for the right words to adequately explain how she felt. "I feel like there is this big hole in my life. I really am having a great time and enjoying myself here, but it's all so confusing. I don't understand what happened to my mom. I can't relax and truly enjoy myself until I do."

Allen's face showed nothing but sympathy as he turned toward Katie. "I don't think either one of us can blame you, Holly. Katie?"

Katie nodded. "It's not that I don't want to answer your questions, Holly. It's just... hard. So much of it was painful for all of us, and I try not to think about it." She sighed. "But tell me what you know, and I'll do my best to fill in the rest."

As they began eating the dinner of lasagna, garlic bread, and salad, Holly told the story as she understood it. Her mother was young and fell for an older guy. The first time she slept with him, she told him she loved him, and he stopped contacting him. After that, she found out she was pregnant and decided to follow him to Denver.

"She said his name was Charlie and then she started referring to him by the letter C in the diary," Holly explained. "The last thing she wrote was that she had told you and you wanted her to stay, get an abortion or something." Holly stabbed her fork into her lasagna, but couldn't bring herself to take a bite. "It was me, wasn't it?"

Katie sighed. "Yes, it was. But I only told her that because she was so young. So was I. It's not that I don't love you," she said, flustered.

"No, no, I'm not upset over that," Holly said shaking her head. Everyone was silent as they ate their dinner. No one looked upset, just curious and supportive. They all were intrigued by the story. "That's not what I'm focused on. First of all, I want to know what happened when she left."

Katie took a bite and slowly chewed it as she thought. "Well, I did wait a little while before I told our parents. I think I gave her most of the day, as far as I remember," she began. "I told them everything. I told them how she'd kept it a secret at first. I was pretty surprised at how well she'd hidden the fact she was seeing an older guy.

"They were as surprised as I was in the beginning, but once the story came together it all started to make sense, such as the way she'd been acting. I didn't even get a chance to tell them right away that she was pregnant. They were beside themselves when I told them she'd run off. Finally, when I told them about the pregnancy, they were stunned into silence." She stopped talking for a moment, her eyes wide and distant.

"What did they do?" Lissa asked quietly.

"What everyone does when you think your child has run away. They called the police. My mother and I started going through Maggie's room looking for clues as to exactly where she was going. We knew she said she was going to Denver, but it's not exactly a small town, you know? So, we searched, hoping to find something that would give us a clue, but we found nothing."

Katie paused before she blinked several times and pulled herself together. "Those first few days were probably the worst. Not knowing if she was okay or not. Wondering if she made it the whole way or if she was lying dead in a ditch somewhere. Our mother took it the worst. She felt responsible for some reason. She kept saying that a mother should have known these things. At the time, I didn't understand." She looked around the table at her children. "But now I do."

"So you guys basically had to sit around and wait for her to turn up?" Holly asked. She found it ironic that she had done much of the same her entire life. Wondering if her mother would come home, or if she'd overdosed somewhere.

"Something like that, but it seems too simplistic to say it that way. We put up flyers, made phone calls. Our parents were making plans to go to Denver themselves before…," Katie stopped and cleared her throat. She swallowed heavily and seemed to struggle with what she was about to say next, "…before my mother collapsed."

"What happened?" Holly asked. She'd wondered from time to time what had happened to her grandmother all those years ago, but so much had happened, she hadn't had a chance to put too much thought into it.

"The doctors told her she had a weak heart and all of the stress she was under wasn't helping her. They kept telling her she needed to relax, but she just couldn't. She kept telling them that she'd relax when Maggie was safely back home." Katie shook her head, a tear slipping down her cheek. She brushed it away before continuing. "She ended up having a heart attack."

Holly gasped. "You mean, my mother caused it?"

"She didn't even know it had happened," Katie said, "until late one night when she called."

It seemed like everyone was holding their breath as they listened. There was the occasional scrape of a fork on a plate or a crunch of bread, but beyond that, there were no sounds.

"It was just a day or so after Mom had died. Maybe longer. The whole thing kind of blurs together in my memory. All I remember is that it was before the funeral. Dad and I were both hurting, losing half of the family in a matter of weeks.

"When the phone rang late one night and Dad answered it, he looked as though he'd heard a ghost. I kept asking him who it was, but he just listened. Then, his face contorted. He said things I'm sure he didn't really mean, but he was just hurting so much. He blamed Maggie for Mom's death. He told her that everything was her fault, and he didn't want to ever see her again. Then he dropped the phone and went to his room. That's when I picked it up," Katie said.

"Grandpa told Aunt Maggie not to come home?" Steven asked.

Katie nodded. "He was hurting. As he saw it, if Maggie hadn't run away, his wife would still be here. I'm not sure if he's ever forgiven himself for what he said that night. He doesn't talk about it."

"What did you say to her when you picked up the phone?" Holly asked.

"I asked her where she was. She said 'Denver, like I said. What is Dad talking about?' That's when it really hit me that she didn't know what had happened to our mother. Dad hadn't said why, he'd just started blaming her. I told her that our mother had been so stressed over her leaving that her weakened heart had given out. That if she hadn't been so selfish, our mother would still be alive.

"I heard her sobbing and when I stopped talking, she told me about what happened when she got to Denver. That she was broke. She'd found Charlie, and he'd slammed the door in her face. He told her to leave him alone, and that he didn't believe the baby was his. She'd hitchhiked out of Denver with a truck driver who had stopped in Cottonwood Springs. She said she was going to try to get the money to come home."

Katie shook her head again and a few more tears slipped down her cheeks. "I was so mad at her then, and honestly, I think I still kind of am. Anyway, I said ugly things to her. I told her we didn't want her here anymore. The last words I ever said to her was that I hoped I never saw her again," a soft sob escaped her lips. "And I didn't."

"She didn't come back for the funeral?" Holly asked sadly. She couldn't imagine not doing everything you could to attend your own mother's funeral.

Katie shook her head. "No. In a way, I'd hoped on the day of the funeral that she would. I think Dad did, too. We both kept looking toward the doors in the church and then at the horizon when we were at the cemetery. But she never showed."

"So that was it?" Holly asked surprised. "She never reached out again?"

"Once," Katie admitted. "She wrote a letter. It was probably almost a year later. Dad threw the letter away without opening it. I think when she didn't show up, it hardened his heart toward her. He's a good man, but everything that happened changed him. We got to where we didn't speak about her for a very long time. Not until we'd heard she'd passed, actually." She took a long drink of water and allowed herself to regain her composure. "I took the letter from the trash and read it."

"What did it say?" Lissa asked, mirroring Holly's thoughts.

"That she was barely able to feed herself, let alone the baby. She wrote about you," she said as she looked at Holly. "She explained how she saw the error of her ways and that she wanted to come home, but she needed money and rehab. She said she'd started doing drugs and wanted to stop, but couldn't do it on her own. I told Dad, but he said she needed to fix her own mess, and he burned the letter. I didn't get a chance to save the return address so I couldn't even respond."

"So, she thought you had turned your back on her," Holly said sadly.

"Well, we pretty much did," Katie admitted, "although I'm not very proud of it. Looking back, I would have done it so much differently. I wouldn't have let her get a head start. I would have gone to her. I would have fought harder. It's just in that moment…," she stopped speaking as her words choked off.

"It's okay," Holly said softly. "You were hurting, too." Holly felt tears pricking her eyes as she thought of the impossible situation her aunt had been in.

Katie nodded as Allen gently rubbed her back. "I was. And I was so hurt and angry that she'd put me in that position. I hoped maybe she'd grow up and see that she messed up. You know, come home and ask for forgiveness. But she never did."

Everyone was silent for a long time, trying to take in what they'd heard. A girl who ran off to follow a man she loved, only to find out he didn't feel the same way towards her and she was carrying his baby. She realized too late that she'd messed up and had hurt the ones she loved in the process. By then, everyone was too shattered and stubborn to apologize.

"Thank you for telling me," Holly finally said.

Katie looked at her niece and smiled weakly at her. "I'm only sorry you had to force it from me. I just didn't want to admit my part in the whole thing. I've felt responsible for all of it for so long that it actually feels good to finally get it out."

"I'm proud of you, honey," Allen said. "That took bravery to admit all of that."

"He's right," Holly said, and Steven and Lissa nodded in agreement.

"Well, I'm here now, and it's because of you, Katie. The family is back together again," Holly said with a reassuring smile.

Katie looked at Holly as if the thought hadn't occurred to her.

"She's right," Steven said. "That was your doing."

Katie smiled, "Thank you. At least I finally did something right."

CHAPTER TWENTY-FIVE

After dinner, Lissa and Steven excused themselves before Katie slipped quietly into the kitchen to put away the leftovers and clean up.

"I feel terrible," Holly finally said to Allen.

He looked at her sympathetically. "I understand why you would, but you really don't need to feel that way."

"How can I not?" Holly asked. She felt the tension rolling around inside her. "I feel like an ungrateful jerk for making her tell me all of that."

"But did you do it to hurt her?" he asked pointedly. He took the last few bites of his lasagna and leaned back in his chair.

"Definitely not," Holly said shaking her head. "But I made her cry."

"Yes, but this is something she's needed to let out. It's been eating at her all these years. I know it has. I've seen it. But she always felt as though her hands were tied. Like she needed to leave it alone and let it take its own course. After your mother died, she was shattered." Allen wiped his mouth with his napkin and watched Holly.

"Lissa and Steven didn't say anything about that," Holly said absently.

"That's because they didn't know. Katie is much stronger than she looks. I'm starting to think most women don't get credit for the strength nobody sees. Especially mothers. But once she heard about your mom and that she'd missed the funeral, she cried most nights when she thought nobody knew," Allen said softly.

"Why? It wasn't her fault if she didn't hear about it in time," Holly questioned.

"I know that, but she still felt as though she should have been there. I don't know how many times I tried to get her to talk about this whole situation, and she just wouldn't. Like you, I didn't want to hurt her, so I let her be, hoping that somewhere along the line she'd open up and talk about it.

"It wasn't until she found out about you and where you were that she stopped crying. It was like she had something else to focus her attention on rather than her grief."

Allen stood up and collected his plate from the table. "You are family. You deserved to know what happened above anyone else. I think you were probably the only person in the world she'd open up to, for just that very reason."

He sighed. "It will all work out, Holly. You'll see. In the meantime, I want you to find some things you want to do around here. We're still going to celebrate. If anything, I think there's even more of a reason to now." He patted her on the shoulder before taking her plate from her and heading to the kitchen.

There was so much to think about. Learning everything she just had, Holly's head felt as though it were spinning. She stood up from the table, slipped silently from the dining room, and headed upstairs. Once in her room, she looked around and let everything sink in.

Her guilt could very well be what had caused Katie to go through the trouble of redoing the room for Holly. Guilt over not being there for her when she was younger, although Holly didn't blame her at all. It wasn't as if she'd known what was going on.

And she'd had her own life to focus on. Getting ready to go to college in St. Louis, then marrying Allen, and making a life of her own like her sister had. The whole situation was just incredibly sad. So much pain just because everyone was too stubborn to reach out and be the first one to apologize. It was senseless suffering that didn't have to be.

Flopping down on the bed, she began to wonder what life would have been like if her mother had made a different choice. What if she'd stayed and never left? Holly would have grown up here in Springfield, surrounded by family and friends. Her mother might even still be here. She might never have turned to drugs and alcohol to numb the pain, which was what Holly was certain she'd done.

There were so many memories of her mother reaching for a bottle when things got tough. Raising a baby when you're still pretty much a child yourself had to have been hard. Not that it was an excuse, but it made her mother less of a villain and more of a real person to her.

Pulling out her phone, she thought about messaging Brigid, but then she decided against it. It was Brigid and Linc's honeymoon. Far better that she just let them enjoy themselves and tell them the news later. Instead, she pulled out a book and changed into something a little more comfortable. For now, all she wanted to do was escape from reality.

Her favorite book series had been put on the back burner for a while, but now she could focus on it again. All the mysteries that occurred in Springfield, both past and present, had been solved, and she could go back to being a kid for a little while longer.

EPILOGUE

Holly couldn't believe how fast the rest of her trip had gone. True to her word, Chloe had moved up the bonfire party so Holly could attend. She'd even made her the guest of honor. There had been a cake and a special crown she'd bought for Holly to wear so everyone would know that she was the one who had saved everything. All that attention had made Holly feel incredibly awkward, but by the end of the night she'd grown somewhat used to it.

There had been fireworks, which everyone loved. Holly wasn't sure she'd ever seen so many big fireworks set off in the same yard before. Growing up she'd been lucky to have sparklers on the Fourth of July. Once Chloe found out, she had Holly lighting them and they all giggled and laughed like they were little kids.

Holly did her best to enjoy the moment, although sometimes she found herself getting sad. Sad that she'd missed this type of family happiness, sad that it took the death of her mother to experience it. But she didn't let it last for long. Instead, she shook off those feelings and redirected her thoughts to all the wonderful and amazing people that had become a new and permanent part of her life.

It was wonderful how inclusive everyone had been. By the end of the night, Holly had become good friends with Chloe and they'd promised to keep in touch. That was also the night that Chloe told everyone she was dating Steven. She'd realized just how much she'd been missing out on by being so strict with herself. She vowed that her senior year was going to be a memorable one. She didn't want to finish up high school with her nose stuck in a textbook all year.

There were more people paired up at the bonfire. Some of the girls they'd investigated had asked the guys they'd had their eye on and they'd said yes. Leah, who wisely didn't come to the party, even got the courage to ask out Jayce, a guy who she'd apparently been wanting to ask out for a long time. Holly had thought it was mind blowing how many girls had allowed their jealousy of Chloe and fear of rejection to stand in the way of asking out their guy of choice.

Katie and Allen had taken everyone out to see the sights just as they'd promised, and Holly had filled her phone with so many photographs that she eventually had to email some of them to herself just to free up more memory in her phone. They visited the Wildlife Museum and Aquarium as well as the drive through caverns. They even took a day trip down to Branson and had a blast listening to and seeing some country music stars. It had been overwhelming, but fun, all rolled into one. All in all, it had been an amazing trip.

Before she left, she was able to visit her grandpa once more. They talked about her mother and in some ways, she felt that a burden had been lifted from his shoulders as well. By the time she'd left, he made her promise to call him every once in a while, so he could keep up with what was going on in her life.

Just the fact that he cared enough to ask her to call him made Holly feel as though her heart could explode. It was all a bit overwhelming for a girl who had gone from having no one to suddenly having an aunt, uncle, cousins, and a grandfather.

When she got back to Cottonwood Springs, she put the photo she'd had taken with him in one of her new frames and placed it prominently on the shelf in her room. He looked so happy and pleased with his arm around her.

"Holly, I think your boxes have arrived," Brigid called from the great room a few days after she'd return to Cottonwood Springs.

Holly had been in her room putting her new pictures in frames and trying to find a place for everything. She hurried out into the hall just as Brigid was opening the door for the delivery man. Holly began to count the boxes as they were being brought in. Before he was finished bringing them in, it seemed as though there were a lot more than she'd remembered.

"This is a lot of boxes," Brigid said, echoing Holly's thoughts. "It looks like Linc moved in all over again," she chuckled.

"I don't remember there being this many," Holly said as she began to unstack them.

"Look, this one has a letter attached to it," Brigid said as she moved one of the boxes. Holly began to pick at the tape that held it down until she was able to lift a corner and pull it off. The handwriting looked familiar and when she opened the letter Holly realized her aunt had written it.

Dear Holly,

We were all so glad to have you come and visit. Anytime you want to come back, you just let us know. It was wonderful getting to know you and hear all about your home in Cottonwood Springs.

You may be thinking that this looks like a lot more stuff than what you had set aside, and it is. Your grandpa was going to write a letter to explain, but his handwriting isn't quite what it used to be, so he asked me to do it for him. Not long after you left, we stumbled upon a little more stuff that we thought you might be interested in.

If you don't want some things, please don't feel as though you have to keep them. These were from your mother and your grandmother. We thought you might like to have them. We tried to make it pretty obvious who they came from. Take your time and go through them slowly. I'm adding a few pages to explain a few things.

Lastly, I want to thank you for making me face my past. It was much easier to just shut the door on what had happened and try to forget it, but obviously I couldn't. But in the end, that did nothing but hurt all of us, your mother most of all. I won't make that mistake again. Thank you for being the catalyst to getting us talking about everything. It was long overdue.

Allen and I have been talking, and we think we'd like to come visit you, someday, not right away, but someday. I'd like to see where you and my sister lived. Please give my love to Brigid and Linc and make sure they get my apology for sending so many boxes. If Brigid is anything like me, she's probably looking at the stack of boxes I sent and wondering where she's going to put it all.

Like I said, you don't need to keep everything. These items are just things. Keep only what makes you happy, because that's what you deserve. Take it from me, holding onto something that brings you pain will never allow you to heal. Only by pulling the bandage off the wound, and looking at it directly, can you really move on.

I'm still sorry for not being there all those years ago when you needed me, but I can't go back in time. If you need anything, anything at all, call me and I will do whatever I can to help. The kids are already asking when they'll get to see you again. Obviously, you've made quite an impression on all of us, and we consider you a part of our family. Don't ever forget that.

With all my love,

Katie

"That's sweet of her," Brigid said after Holly finished reading the letter aloud. "And she's right, that was the first thing I thought when I saw how many boxes there were. Linc's going to be surprised when he gets back home."

"I'll get them moved into my room here in a few. Katie's probably right. I should go through them slowly, so I can really take in each item. You never know what I might find."

"That's very true," Brigid said as she pulled Holly into a hug.

"Don't worry about them being out here. They're not bothering me. Take all the time you need. You can spread them all out if you like. It's interesting to see where you came from, and I'll learn right along with you."

Holly smiled at Brigid. "Thank you. For everything."

"No thanks necessary. You said you found out that Chloe's best friend was the one who framed her?" Brigid asked as she knelt down to scratch Jett on the head.

"Yeah, Lissa and Steven said Chloe and Leah have at least started talking to each other again. They don't know if they'll ever be best friends again, but at least for now they're being civil to one another," Holly said as she sat down on the floor by one of the boxes.

Jett lumbered over to her and sat on her lap, inviting her to pet him. She laughed as he almost pushed her over. "Geeze, Jett. I've been home a couple days now. I've already told you I missed you a million times. What more do you want from me?"

"I'd say he wants to hear it a million and one times," Brigid said with a laugh. "You know, I had a wonderful honeymoon, and it was a great trip, but I'm very glad to be home and back to normal."

"Me, too," Holly said. "Missouri was beautiful, and I had a ton of fun, but Cottonwood Springs is my home. I'm glad to be here."

"Honey, no one is happier than I am that you're here," Brigid said, as she hugged Holly while a warm tear of happiness trickled down her cheek.

Paperbacks & Ebooks for FREE

Go to www.dianneharman.com/freepaperback.html and get your FREE copies of Dianne's books and favorite recipes immediately by signing up for her newsletter.

Once you've signed up for her newsletter you're eligible to win three paperbacks. One lucky winner is picked every week. Hurry before the offer ends!

ABOUT THE AUTHOR

Dianne lives in Huntington Beach, California, with her husband, Tom, a former California State Senator, and her boxer dog, Kelly. Her passions are cooking, reading, and dogs, so whenever she has a little free time, you can either find her in the kitchen, playing with Kelly in the back yard, or curled up with the latest book she's reading.

Her award winning books include:

Cedar Bay Cozy Mystery Series

Cedar Bay Cozy Mystery Series - Boxed Set

Liz Lucas Cozy Mystery Series

Liz Lucas Cozy Mystery Series - Boxed Set

High Desert Cozy Mystery Series

High Desert Cozy Mystery Series - Boxed Set

Northwest Cozy Mystery Series

Northwest Cozy Mystery Series - Boxed Set

Midwest Cozy Mystery Series

Midwest Cozy Mystery Series - Boxed Set

Jack Trout Cozy Mystery Series

Cottonwood Springs Cozy Mystery Series

Coyote Series

Midlife Journey Series

Red Zero Series, Black Dot Series

The Holly Lewis Mystery Series

Newsletter

If you would like to be notified of her latest releases please go to www.dianneharman.com and sign up for her newsletter.

Website: www.dianneharman.com,
Blog: www.dianneharman.com/blog
Email: dianne@dianneharman.com

PUBLISHING 4/17/19

MURDER AT THE ALAMO

BOOK FIVE OF

THE COTTONWOOD SPRINGS COZY MYSTERIES

http://getbook.at/MATA

Al's past is catching up with him...40 years in the mob and karma has his number.

He's a marked man, but a tip-off buys him some time. Can he catch his would-be murderer before they catch up with him?

It's a game of cat and mouse...will Al live to see his new husky puppy Spike grow up? Or will Red be lying vigil by his coffin?

Find out in the latest nail-biting installment of the Northwest Cozy Mystery Series by a two-time USA Today Bestselling Author.

Open your smartphone, point and shoot at the QR code below. You will be taken to Amazon where you can pre-order 'Murder at the Alamo'.

(Download the QR code app onto your smartphone from the iTunes or Google Play store in order to read the QR code below.)

Made in the USA
Columbia, SC
28 February 2020